D0765201

An Answer from the Silence

THE GERMAN LIST

MAX FRISCH

An Answer from the Silence

A STORY FROM THE MOUNTAINS

WITH AN AFTERWORD BY PETER VON MATT

TRANSLATED BY MIKE MITCHELL

Seagull
BOOKS

CALCUTTA LONDON NEW YORK

GOETHE-INSTITUT

This publication was supported by a grant
from the Goethe-Institut India

Seagull Books 2011

Antwort aus der Stille: Eine Erzählung aus den Bergen
First published in German by Verlags-Anstalt, Stuttgart 1937
© Suhrkamp Verlag, Berlin, 2009

First published in English by Seagull Books, 2011
English translation © Mike Mitchell, 2011

ISBN-13   978 1 9064 9 792 7

British Library Cataloguing-in-Publication Data
A catalogue record for this book is available
from the British Library

Typeset by Seagull Books, Calcutta, India
Printed at Leelabati Printers, Calcutta, India

CONTENTS

There could hardly be a better day for walking, blue sky and not too hot. The clouds, like cotton wool, are hanging motionless over the valley, the grasshoppers chirping in the meadows. It is still summer, only the shimmer of light over the fields already has a golden softness and a single brown-edged leaf lying on the path is enough to bring on thoughts of autumn, even though everything is still green, the brightly coloured butterflies are fluttering through the air and the ripening corn is still standing on the slopes.

For hours now the walker has hardly allowed himself a rest; he has taken off his shirt and is carrying his rucksack on his bare shoulders, which are brown and gleaming. It's a heavy rucksack, loaded with a rope and crampons, a sleeping bag and tent; he is carrying pitons as well, and anyone meeting him would see straightaway that this walker with the upright gait and swinging his ice-axe clearly has something big planned.

But no one meets him.

It is a quiet and lonely mountain valley. Now and again the stream can be heard thundering through the gorge, or the route leads past the high rocks where the water pours down in silvery drifts of spray.

It's all still as it was, thirteen years ago. Then he had been walking with his older brother, who showed him various things, explaining for example how such a valley came to be formed, how the old glaciers had slowly ground out a wide trench, just like a carpenter's plane, of which scrape marks of the glaciers on the rocks were evidence, and if you looked along the valley you could see the terraces of an older, higher valley bottom. Only then, his grown-up brother had said, had the stream come and sawn out the narrow gorges, over many thousands of years, of course.

Seeing the rock, the solitary walker recalls all that now. At the time he was still a boy, with the youthful feeling that your life is stretching out in front of you almost endlessly, and perhaps it was here, on this spot, that for the first time he had felt as short-lived as a mayfly—

Thirteen years ago.

At one point a jolting, creaking cart comes and you have to step to one side as long as the dust is swirling up and descending on the meadows in clouds of white.

The solitary walker also remembers the little spring beside the path farther on; its lively babbling is no older now and this time he again takes a drink of the ice-cold water that sometimes simply stops running, only to gurgle and bubble once more all the more merrily. It brings exquisite refreshment to his forehead when he holds it under the pipe; he also dips his brown arms in the mossy wooden trough a second time, before picking up his ice-axe. Soon the black drops on his boots have disappeared under the dust again.

Perhaps he doesn't even know himself why he's not allowing himself to rest, even though he actually has plenty of time. Often he just keeps his eyes fixed on his boots as they walk, not looking to either side, like someone who has an important goal ahead, or at least believes he has, and is concentrating on that alone . . .

The countryside around is becoming more and more deserted; there is scarcely even a hut to be seen. The fields are abuzz with noon and later, at the hottest part of the day, a dull rumbling can be heard echoing somewhere above the valley, a rockfall in the mountains, as there always is at that hour.

That is the same as thirteen years ago as well.

Or perhaps the solitary walker is thinking back. It's a long valley and thirteen years is a long time and he keeps going farther and farther back into his memory. Some things make him smile, a faint smile, either from embarrassment or unacknowledged envy; it was at this wooden bridge that he told his grown-up brother, who had just got engaged, in youthfully open and impudent tones, that getting married was ordinary and he, the seventeen-year-old, would never get married, for he wasn't an ordinary person but an artist or an inventor or something like that. It was the first time he had told anyone that, back then on this wooden bridge, and his grown-up brother had asked him what kind of artist he was, what kind of work he was doing. And that was a question that had cut the boy he then was to the quick, for so far he had not done anything. You'd just had the feeling you weren't a person like all the rest, like your big brother, for example, who was engaged and whom he despised for that reason as the epitome of ordinariness . . .

His way sometimes takes him through woodlands full of a mossy coolness and smelling of mushrooms or resin. The branches are hung with grey-green lichen, like ancient beards swaying gently in the wind, and now and again he keeps getting a view out over the valley sinking in a blue haze.

Later his brother got married and emigrated to Africa, where he has a farm and lots of children. Meanwhile he, the younger one, continued hoping and planning while his youth simply melted away. Being an inventor naturally came to nothing, despite all the days he spent up in the attic, and then he tried acting, then painting, then playing the violin. And eventually the day came when you simply ran away from school, because you might make discoveries as a great explorer; but the only thing he discovered was that he had nowhere near enough money and that it was another mistake, and you were often in despair, as is right and proper for extraordinary people, but he never took his own life. You could still tell yourself: you're only twenty, everything's still possible. And how proud you were that everything was still possible! Later it was: twenty-five's no age at all, and you liked reading about people who had achieved nothing at twenty-five, which was something out of the ordinary, and who those around did not believe had this or that achievement in them. True, you still didn't know in what field your future achievements would lie, but in the meantime you wore ties and hats of a style that would never occur to an ordinary citizen, and even if at times you were afraid you might be ridiculous, or perhaps even crazy, more ridiculous and stupid and worthless and worse than anyone else on earth, it was a painful thought but not without its comfort; at least it gave you the feeling that it that made you a special person, perhaps a criminal, and it was only when you failed to achieve anything by way of misdeeds that others could not do equally well, that a new and more despairing fear set in that your extraordinary achievement might not happen. Simply not happen. From that point on everything you undertook was marked by haste, by impatience and by a feverish ambitiousness, which is rarely fruitful. You really cannot believe that all the longing, all the youthful confidence, all the emotion and all the proud words are simply nothing, fruitless and ordinary. It must eventually come to pass, he still believes that, even if he is slowly growing older and more guarded in what he says. Such things must come in their own good time, you've slowly come to see that and learnt to be patient, even if you find it difficult— especially among people who judge you by your present and not by your future. But you remain silent and wait, and while you're waiting you do what ordinary people do; of course, you do it with a secret smile because you know that you're only pretending and that you aren't an ordinary person, you know that in fact you're waiting, just waiting for things to start moving, for that special gift, for fulfilment, for meaning . . .

By this time the valley has become narrower and steeper, with nothing but a packhorse track, and between the rust-red pines on the steep slope the bluish glimmer of the glacier can already be seen, a wide, torn tongue hanging down and getting thinner and thinner, then the rushing of the stream, the higher you climb.

But when you're walking by yourself, all kinds of thoughts keep going through your mind. It's as if you've got a seventeen-year-old walking beside you, asking you questions as if you owed him an explanation, as if you had to tell yourself you've successfully passed all your exams, with very good marks even, that soon you're going to be a teacher yourself, that you're a Ph.D. and a lieutenant in the Swiss Army and engaged . . .

At one point when he's sitting on a rock, his open rucksack between his feet, he holds his empty cup in his hand for quite a while as if he's forgotten he's thirsty; it's beside a bubbling, foaming stream plunging across the path, and he looks back down the hazy valley where the shadows are already rising.

So that's my life, he keeps thinking and it seems to him it's no life at all, simply an existence.

Later he holds his cup under a jet of water, making it spurt up, and empties it twice, then he watches a bird of prey circling over the cliffs, silently, in great loops, almost without beating its wings. The sky is already getting paler as evening approaches and over the scythed meadows, which slope steeply down the side of the valley, there is a moist, gossamer-thin veil, hardly visible, but you can sense the passing of another year . . .

Once, after he has slung his rucksack back over his shoulders and started climbing again, he meets a local coming down the steep path leading a mule carrying a swaying wooden pack-saddle on its skinny back and always walking on the outer edge of the path, as is their way; the dust swirling up under its hoofs floats out over the precipice for a long time, gleaming in the evening sun like a glowing pall of smoke.

After that the solitary walker does not allow himself to rest again until he reaches the spur with the wooden cross where you suddenly have an extensive view out over the whole valley and up to the mountain, which he can see in his mind's eye all the time—but when the great pile is actually there, in front of him, it's simply immense, exceeding all memories. Its peak towers above drifting clouds. You can see how jagged the ridge is and at the moment the rocks, often sheer faces, are like glowing embers. But that is changing with every moment and soon it is just a fading glimmer. Later it has completely gone and the whole mountain is like dark cinders and the drifting clouds grey ash blowing in the wind.

But the walker is still there, sitting against the wooden cross, looking through his binoculars at the North Ridge, which no man has ever climbed . . .

His heart is pounding.

It's a good thing no one knows what he intends to do; they would tell him it was madness or suicide, and they wouldn't be telling him anything he didn't know already.

By the time he has put his binoculars away it is already getting dark; but from this cross it's only an hour to the tiny village, from which the faint, forlorn jingle of cow bells can now be heard, and to the inn, where he intends to spend the night, perhaps another two or three days as well . . .

For he also knows that the challenge he has set himself demands serious work and patience. He will put in further practice on the rocks so that he can hope with confidence for the success without which he will not return home. It is his last attempt and no one is going to stop him, neither with pleas nor with warnings. There comes a point when you have to realize your youthful hopes, if they are not to become a laughing stock, realize them with a manly deed, and you will see whether or not the things you had believed for so many years were simply delusions of grandeur. There comes a point when you have to take the risk: the deed or death, for he has sworn a vow that he cannot, will not stand the kind of life he is starting out on, the life of an average person—never!

The inn is still the way it was thirteen years ago, the rooms of unpainted wood, the window frames weather-worn and outside, when you open the shutter, the plaster falls off in great lumps. And on the grassy terrace below the front you can see the guests taking the air after dinner; you can look over the grey shingle roofs of the little village across the darkening valley to the mountains, which are now like pale, brittle porcelain.

All that is also the way it was thirteen years ago.

As is the fact that the mountain guide, who has grown a beard in the meantime, is sitting at his round table, as he does every evening, together with the little old postman, who likes his glass of red wine while he leaves his mule tied to a tree; and sometimes there are hunters there as well with marmots, or once there's even a chamois hanging on the wooden balustrade; then the white ladies come and stroke its dead coat, while the gentlemen take their cigars out of their mouth and look for the bullet hole or want to know where and how the beautiful animal was shot.

That is the way evenings are up there.

Later they go back in because it's getting cool outside; perhaps they leaf through the visitors' book, but the new arrival hasn't put his name in yet, so they simply call him the odd fellow, either because he came to dinner in his mountain garb or because he disappeared immediately afterwards and didn't show his face for the rest of the evening.

They play the game with the cup and the mice again, the one the young Danish woman showed them, and again they enjoy themselves immensely; the way she laughs, this foreign woman, everyone who's there just has to join in, even the older gentlemen who are only watching, once a chair is even broken when someone throws himself back with laughter, a new chair's brought and the game continues . . .

While all this is going on the new arrival, the one they call the odd fellow, is already in bed trying to get to sleep.

They were to wake him at four and have his packed lunch ready, he told the hotel servant downstairs, and his rucksack is on the chair, with everything in it so that he won't lose any time in the morning.

Isn't life good, he thinks, when you're tired and you know why you're waking up the next morning. It's so rare to know that, you're always getting up to an empty and sterile existence, sometimes you even think you can't stand it any longer. But you can be in deep despair, you can throw yourself down on the table, sometimes you even feel like hitting your head against the wall to make all the thoughts inside it come spurting out—eventually, at some point or other, a sleep will come that is stronger than everything else, stronger than our thoughts and our despair, a sleep that simply postpones everything and erases thought before it becomes fatal. Yet you know very well that sleep doesn't solve anything, that it's just going to strengthen us for further despair, and that the next day you'll still be stuck in the same place and you'll still have to get up again and continue this aimless existence, without belief and without a goal, without meaning, without anything, without a vocation, simply in order to grow older, emptier and even more desperate . . .

But now things are going to change, now he knows why they're going to wake him next morning, and he doesn't have to shudder at the thought of waking, now he has a goal he can think about, a goal he's determined to believe in, a goal for which he has to get up!

Meanwhile he's taking a long time to get to sleep and it strikes twelve, down in the village, while he's still lying there awake—

Perhaps he's thinking of his fiancée, sitting at home and crying perhaps, since she has no idea where he's gone, perhaps he's thinking that a loving woman is always a burden because love alone cannot redeem a man; the woman knows that too, but still she expects it, always secretly expects it, even if she sometimes says the opposite and, anyway, how can she understand since basically she's all love; how can she understand that with the best will in the world she can never satisfy and hold him, even if he can perhaps satisfy her, and that

11

therefore for him there's no standing still in love, no satiety, you always have to take one step further, whether to manly unfaithfulness or manly deeds.

*

The next morning the sky is almost cloudless again and the guests, who come down with their walking sticks, have their breakfast on the dazzling white tables outside . . .

Some have already set off.

In the meadow above, a red dress can be seen; it's the young foreign woman, already she's picked a whole bouquet of flowers. And the black goats are grazing on the edge of the forest again, the scattered tinkling of their bells can be heard every morning; they slowly make their way uphill, driven by a little girl. She has a large branch in her hand; sometimes she throws a stone as well, to make the animals obey.

It's no longer early by the time the odd fellow throws open his shutters. The ceaseless rushing noise he took for pouring rain when he was woken at four o'clock is still there; it's the stream that can be heard from down in the valley. And the mountains are so magnificently clear, the ridges, so white and pure, set off against a spotless blue and everything already shining in the transparent, almost blazing, sunshine of the late morning, the time when you ought to be on the summit!

But getting annoyed won't change anything, it won't change the fact that you've overslept, that more time has been wasted . . .

It's getting hot. The grasshoppers are chirping in the grass again, they leap aside at every step, often they're the length of your finger and jump up almost as high as your head. At the forest edge it's the bees humming. And sometimes there's the rustle of a lizard that's been sunning itself on a warm rock or the gleam of a butterfly that disappears in a fluttering zigzag, red or yellow, and the distant slopes blur in the quivering, shimmering blue haze.

It's a very ordinary footpath the odd fellow has to make do with today. It goes beside one of the many little rivulets there are in the area; sometimes they run along a wooden channel, sometimes a course has been cut through the rock, and then they're trickling and glittering over golden brown pebbles again, always across the slope and usually there's a path beside them which is marvellous for a stroll, following the soft, secret murmuring, the silvery tones that haven't changed in thirteen years . . .

Perhaps it was one of these paths he had dreamt of the previous night, with his late father walking behind him. There was another man with them too, a colonel whose face sometimes reminded you of the innkeeper, sometimes of an old swimming instructor, anyway, the look on that colonel's face kept getting more and more reproachful when you were supposed to show him a stone you'd found, the scrape mark of a glacier, evidence of everything you'd been saying, and when you opened your hand, it was empty and nothing came of what he wanted to explain to his pupils; he was standing in front of his future class in a nightshirt that was far too short and eventually they all burst out laughing . . .

A stupid dream.

At one point he watches a farmer's wife watering her steep meadow; the little child she carried in a basket on her back is now sitting between the two shaggy goats and the gaunt woman, whose face looks like a hard, dark-brown woodcut, dams the little stream with a flat stone: the water pours down the slope in a glittering cascade, combing the grass flat. Then she takes a short-handled hoe and goes along the little gullies, whose purpose is to spread the water over the dry meadow, checking that there are no blockages. When she's finished, she goes and stops up the gaps with stones and moss, so that no water is wasted; the whole village depends on a little stream like that and there's a strict weekly schedule they have to stick to, strict regulation for a modest existence.

The wooden sluice is still there as well and he's pleased about that as he stands on the bouncy plank; he fell into it once when he was trying to get his father's walking stick out of the icy water. But it's strange, everything seems smaller to him; even in the inn he felt the large veranda had shrunk, also a boulder on the slope where his brother gave him his first rock-climbing lessons, everything seemed bigger back then.

Finally he comes to the big stream, the noise of which he heard during the night, and to the old mill, which was abandoned and in ruins even thirteen years ago. Today you can still see the collapsed roof, covered in spider's webs, and the rotten water-wheel lying among thistles and nettles. Beside it the water thunders and foams. And now the lonely walker is beyond the cultivated area, standing on a large rock in the middle of the raging water. He's looking for the dam he built to create a large lake when he was a boy; he remembers people telling him he was a born architect and they patted him on the back and told him he'd be a great man when he grew up. But of course since then the stream has swept everything away, rocks and branches, nothing could resist it, nothing at all.

Later he sits on a mossy boulder among pines and neglected fir trees, the lower branches of which hang down in the stream, staring at the ever-changing, foaming water, the silver fan where it cascades over flat stones; sometimes a whole veil of spray drifts across and all the time you can hear a dull rumbling, as if from a distance, somewhere under the sparkling water.

Perhaps it wasn't a good idea to come to this valley, everything seems smaller, the time he was perhaps looking for has disappeared from it . . .

He only notices when his hands have already finished: he has cut a boat out of a piece of blood-red bark, such as is everywhere on the ground around him. His first impulse is the throw away the childish toy in his hand, but instead he continues to carve at it, very carefully so that the brittle bark doesn't split, and he even manages to make a hole in it for a tiny mast before launching his little creation. It's slightly lopsided as it floats and an eddy makes it go round in a circle. He probably smiles, as he folds up his pocketknife, half embarrassed, half contemptuous, until his boat is about to float away and he grasps it quickly, not the way you would rescue something you despise.

Evening is already approaching when some people come over the bridge. He obviously doesn't hear their voices . . .

They must have been watching him for a quarter of an hour: standing in the stream, his sleeves rolled up so he can pick stones out of the water, and in the little lake he's dammed up with rocks and branches the childish boat can also be seen sailing round merrily; he appears to be completely absorbed in his task, just now he's gathering the pine cones he needs to block the holes between the stones and whistling as he goes about it. And he still hasn't noticed them, the audience close by on the bridge; the young foreign woman in the red dress is with them and she stays watching the man at play for quite a while after her two companions have moved on and are already disappearing in the trees over on the other side—

At that moment it so happens that the dam-builder has to brush his hair out of his face again and looks up as he does so. And is thunderstruck. The roar of the water makes impossible a casual remark that would resolve the situation and all they can do is stare at each other, the woman watching on the bridge and the man standing in the foaming stream like a little boy and throwing away the pine cones he has gathered as if they were stolen goods.

And later, when he's alone again, he demolishes the dam with one kick, as if he suddenly feels ashamed even before these mute stones.

*

But of course Irene, as the young foreign woman is called, did not make as much of this meeting as he perhaps imagines. She's a bright, cheerful, healthy young woman, who gets up early to pick flowers and sings as she strolls through the twilit woods.

She's there with the sister and brother-in-law, has been for four weeks and it's often pretty boring for her. Especially when her brother-in-law, as is the way with almost all men, keeps talking about his work. Then she just nods and whistles, or chews on stalks she plucks as she passes, or if there's a large fungus by the path, a chanterelle, for example, she hits it with her walking stick, smashing it and setting off a cloud of dust. She has to be doing something and her sister, who is actually younger, has often criticized her for her impatience. Irene can't even read a book, she says, and she's right. When they sit down on a bench or in the grass, it does sometimes happen that Irene picks up the book she's been given, but it only needs an insect to come along for her to forget the invented story and leave it to the wind to continue turning the pages. She allows the beast to crawl over the letters and talks to the insects, in Danish, of course, even to the ugly ones; and then she puts cunning obstacles in their way, which they have to overcome, and if an insect can't free itself by the time she's counted twelve, it's squashed with a stone and killed, and only the brave insects are given their freedom and their life, as a just reward, for everything has to be earned. It seems, though, that best of all Irene likes playing with the children, they always run to meet her when they see them coming back to the inn and then, yes, Irene does have the patience she otherwise lacks; they are the innkeeper's children, two lively little lads who jabber away in French, Irene can hardly understand a word but they get on fine together. She's shown them how to weave baskets, and recently they went gathering bilberries and they all came back with black mouths; every day Irene thinks up something new, once she cut their fingernails and their laughter echoed round the building. And in the evening she has to put the two little rascals to bed herself since otherwise they refuse to let their friend go; then, depending on how they've behaved, there's a kiss up here or a smack down there.

That's the way Irene is.

She's not the kind of person who's given to introspection and after dinner, when they sit round the fire and play the boisterous game with the cup and mice she certainly has no idea that there's someone in the inn who takes her ringing laughter very personally. Perhaps she's already completely forgotten the day that's just passed. She's a woman, she lives in momentary states, not thoughts, so what is it to her, in this state of merry play, that in the meantime the odd fellow, who that afternoon was standing in the rushing stream trying to rebuild the days of his childhood, has signed the visitors' book as Dr Leuthold? She sits there in her long evening dress concentrating solely, as the moment demands, on trying to catch the toy mice with the cup, with no idea that she is playing a hidden role, that she is influencing a man's decisions two storeys higher up . . .

The next morning, when she comes down to breakfast again and is about to sit down at the white tables, dazzling in the sunshine, all the guests are standing round the telescope and everyone wants to look at the cliffs that are just coming into the morning sun. There's someone on the rock face! they say, and even the German, who has just been looking through the telescope, thinks it's quite something. Then the ladies, full of horrified curiosity, want to have a look as well. He's been climbing for three hours already, the innkeeper tells them, and then they also learn that this route hasn't been done for four years because there's always a danger of falling rocks. And that it can only be climbed by an awkward chimney, which is vertical with almost no holds, and if you don't find it there's no hope of reaching the top.

It's an exciting morning.

Irene has a look through the telescope as well: in a circle, the edges of which shimmer in all the colours of the rainbow, she can see the sunlit, bone-yellow rock face, perhaps the height of the wall of a tall cathedral, and on it the tiny man, moving only very slowly; you can clearly see him feeling his way, checking the holds before he takes a big step and slowly pushes himself up. And then once more looking around, for a very long time, before going back down and trying somewhere else; you can even see him taking out stones and dropping them, in absolute silence of course, which makes it seem unreal and eerie, and once he crosses a smooth section by jamming his hands in a sloping crack and swinging, and then he's back in the shade again and for a long time you can't see what he's doing . . .

They spend the whole morning watching.

Every time she steps back from the telescope, Irene can hear her heart beating; but still she has no idea that she's the one who drove him to the cliff, to his crazy venture, as they generally term it.

The telescope is only abandoned when the bell for lunch has rung three times and the ascent is temporarily relegated to conversation; you can not only hear the different opinions—approving or disapproving, confident or pessimistic—while you eat your soup, above all you can hear the clatter of cutlery, louder than usual, as if today people were eating particularly quickly so the man wouldn't fall before they were back at the telescope . . .

But he doesn't fall.

Strange, the silence that greets a panting rock-climber on the summit, a silence that hasn't been waiting for him, a silence that ignores his arrival and makes him feel almost embarrassed, now, when he's achieved what he set out to do and would like to feel proud, a silence that knows nothing of ambition . . .

Finally he unbuckles his rucksack.

The white mountains all round are as dazzling as on the first day, when God created light, they jag up into the high, blue heaven, as clear and sharp and pointed as crystals, as far as the eye can see, like God's upright, silvery handwriting inscribed on the luminous edge of this world.

Later, after he's rubbed sun-cream on his forehead, neck and arms and put the pot away, perhaps he thinks for a moment of the young foreign woman, who saw him in the stream the previous day; but only for a moment—

It is as if this silence over the world dissolves all thought; you can hear nothing but your heart beating, or now and then the wind whistling past your ears. And if a black chough should happen to glide round the rock and then disappear with a hoarse croak, there still remains the lonely silence, which envelops all life and swallows every cry as if it had never been, this nameless silence, which is perhaps God, perhaps nothingness.

And which the climber does not find easy to bear.

So then, in order to have something to do, he takes out his binoculars and has another look at the North Ridge, wedging himself in the rocks so that he can be perfectly still; it really is a monstrous ridge if you survey it from close to, step by step. There are vertical and even overhanging faces, and no one knows if there are any holds. He sharpens the focus of his binoculars, but of course the holds don't show, all that can be made out is an overhanging cornice, which interrupts the ridge in several places, and there really are individual needles of rock, as if the devil had thought them up, deadly ornaments.

When he lowers his binoculars he hasn't examined half the ridge yet.

But orders are orders and there's no grumbling about why he, of all men, should attempt this ridge that no one has climbed; no doubting and no asking whether it really is enough for a man to simply set himself a goal, no matter whether it is pleasing to God or merely to our fellow men, no matter whether it really is an expression of his longing or just of his determination . . .

Orders are orders.

As it is, he soon set about the descent; he spent scarcely a quarter of an hour on the summit, even though it was so magnificent, scarcely a quarter of an hour . . .

Perhaps a very clear conscience was needed to withstand this very pure silence; otherwise it might be that everything you have spent your whole life very carefully building up and maintaining would collapse and disintegrate in an hour, a heroic ambition might perhaps reveal itself as vain, as a mere excuse, it might be that if you sat there long enough all that was left would be the dark stain, some fundamental lie of the heart which you suspect and have always feared and tried to cover up a hundred times because you simply do not have the courage, the courage to openly acknowledge it, to truly change.

Towards evening, when he comes back down to the valley, the sky is overcast; the shadows of the clouds are like cloths moving over the icy peaks, which have a faint golden glow; they also creep up the slopes and it's beautiful to watch: the moving clouds and the shadows and the forests, now turning brown and mauve. The valley is filled with a bluish evening haze and sometimes the sun manages to break through again, casting its slanting rays through the air like a bundle of silver spears.

Irene is sitting in her deckchair; and why should she not speak to the climber as he appears on the terrace and looks at the weather?

He's been lucky to get the last fine day, she says, and asks whether he had a good view.

'Oh, yes!' He's standing by the railing, his left hand in his trouser pocket, smoking his pipe, and he's certainly not unhappy that she saw him on the climb, she who the previous day saw him standing in the stream like a little boy, playing with his boat made out of a piece of bark. You have to say that it was a daring climb he did today, and it's glorious to see the clouds rolling across it; it's almost impossible to tell what is mountain and what cloud now that everything's glowing and merging.

He's presumably got something big planned? she asks as she packs her bag, since it's getting cool outside on the terrace. He takes his pipe out of his mouth:

'Yes—the North Ridge.'

He says it very modestly, very simply and naturally. But the young foreign woman doesn't know what it means; she doesn't know she's the first person he's told, and perhaps he's telling her so that there's no way back for him; she just gets her knitting together, very calmly, as if he'd been talking about some ordinary outing—

So he says himself that the North Ridge was not supposed to be easy, at least no one had ever climbed it yet.

And he wants to climb it now?

With a vigorous sweep she combs back her hair that the wind has dishevelled and smiles, not a mocking or doubting smile, just a very neutral one; then she puts the comb away.

'But why?' she asks.

He just looks at her . . .

You can't say she's positively beautiful; she has large, very white teeth, a brown face and her hair has a pale sheen; it's probably just her eyes that make her face so disconcerting, her swift, alert eyes with an almost brazen, very direct and often high-spirited expression.

But why . . . ?

He still hasn't found an answer to her uninhibited question; he just shrugs his shoulders in a half embarrassed, half dismissive gesture, since she appears to know nothing of such matters, then he puffs at his pipe again while she gathers her things.

She's sure he wants to get in the newspapers, she says, looking at him and laughing out loud, not at all malicious, just very frank . . .

Then the bell goes for dinner.

*

As it happens, the young foreign woman's right; the next day it really is raining, in fact it's pouring down. The mist is swirling up out of the valley, as if potatoes were being boiled, and pouring over the slopes in swathes of grey, veiling all the mountains.

They spend the whole day sitting in the lounge, where there's a fire. Sometimes a log crackles or just hisses if it's still damp. Otherwise it's very quiet, everyone occupying themselves in their own way and if someone speaks, they do so in a whisper, as if it were a waiting room:

It appears that she's playing with the children again, down on the ground floor, sometimes it's loud and boisterous, chairs can be heard falling over and doors being slammed, the children shouting and squealing; and you can hear Irene laughing too, as if it were her own children she was chasing.

Why?

It is the most discourteous question one can ask of life . . .

One of them's playing chess, another's reading the stock market report and a third, with an equally serious expression, is observing the grasshoppers he's collected in his green tin, while others are resting their chins on their hands and brooding over a crossword with almost passionate intensity.

Why?

A person has to do something, or should he spend his whole life just sitting there, staring into space and wondering what God, in his unfathomable boredom, thought He was doing when He created man?

You can also stare at the crackling fire and guess which log will start to burn first, or count the fringes on the tablecloth, you can listen to your pulse or ponder over the intertwining pattern of the carpet and work out what it would be like if it were different. Or you can read the newspaper, which always has very important things to say, or smoke and think your own thoughts, or have exciting conversations and listen to yourself. There is so much you can do. Or you can devote yourself to study, for example you can throw yourself into some science, you can investigate the shards of past races, or work out when two stars will be closest to each other, you can determine how hot a flash of lightning is or concern yourself with fish whose scales no one has perhaps yet examined, oh, there are so many scales and shards and stars, and you can die before you've counted everything, catalogued it and ordered it into species . . .

Why?

Or you can become a poet, you can go round with furrowed brow, despairing because you can't find a very important rhyme, you can ponder and ponder and forget the passing hours over a line, forget the days and years, you can forget your whole life and wrap up nothingness in empty words . . .

Having something to occupy you is everything.

And why shouldn't someone else go and travel all the way round the world in somersaults or have the ambition of climbing some north ridge or other?

You have to have something to do!

Sometimes the fire collapses because another log has burnt to ashes; then someone takes the tongs and puts another log on, so that the fire doesn't go out, so that it will keep crackling for another half hour . . .

There are moments when you feel like leaping up and thumping the table with your fist, making everyone start! And then asking them if they know why they do this or that? Moments when you feel like tearing off their faces, with their calm, confident expressions, just tearing them off like paper masks! And asking them if they have any idea why they bother to put on an expression in this world, why they get up and get dressed in the morning, why they read and work and play, what the point of it all is? Or perhaps even they have no idea and in the end they only go on living because it's the done thing, because living's an old-established custom? And because no one will admit to the profound emptiness and boredom that yawns behind everything, and because all the others put on such serious expressions and behave as if they knew a meaning, a why—God, you feel like getting up and thumping the table with your fist to give everyone a start and make them be honest!

But who's going to stand up . . .

Outside it's raining incessantly; with the water making rivulets all over the window panes you can hardly see out and all you can hear is a faint, grey, indeterminate swooshing noise.

In the afternoon Irene plays billiards with the odd fellow who, as it happens, turns out to be an ace. Irene can only marvel. When it's his turn he sometimes makes cannons by the dozen, so then she wanders round the room and stands by the window, where the rain is still running down like quicksilver.

It's an absolute flood, she says.

Sometimes the balls hit each other so hard they almost jump over the edge and she's surprised herself how she manages to make cannons without long and earnest consideration of the shot, but just like that, the way she feels—

Does she like reading books? he asks once when he stops by the little table with her book on it and she, the way women do, just answers by asking him the same question.

'No!' he says with a very decisive laugh, flicking through it. 'At least not good books which are intended to replace real life and save us the bother of doing things ourselves.' For in books, he goes on, things always get done, one way or another, and that's why people read them, there's always a clear course of events, nothing's pointless, even if everything turns out differently, and nothing fizzles out, everything has a secret place in the order of things, sometimes even a meaning—

'And you don't like that?' she asks as she makes a cannon and goes round the table with fluid movements.

Real life is so different, he says . . .

His at least, he thinks. In his life there's no clear course of events to be seen, no underlying thread, it just drags on, with no defining moments, no great deeds, passion fades to become a mood and his decisions are like sand quietly running through his fingers: you keep on picking up another handful and when you open your hand, there's nothing there, you're in despair and even that fades, like hope and jubilation and pain and everything, like your whole life.

Then it's his turn again.

There's no doubt who is going to win, but apart from their game of billiards this young foreign woman, who keeps wandering round and whistling, is not an easy person to deal with. She has a way of asking questions, for example, how old is he?

'Coming up for thirty,' he mutters.

And what does he do?

And just as in an interrogation, he has to answer, while he walks round the table, keeping his eyes on the balls, as if everything else were of minor importance.

What, he's a teacher?

At that she stops and looks at him as he's never been looked at before, a wide-eyed, unflinching, sympathetic look, and says that in that case he must be terribly fond of children.

'Terribly—yes.'

But now she doesn't believe his contemptuous grin any more, no, nor does it make any difference to her that he goes on to say that he could just as well have become a painter or a chimney-sweep; there are some people who can do anything because they have no particular vocation, so it's best if such people sacrifice themselves for the general good, as a teacher in peacetime or a lieutenant in wartime . . .

But Irene just smiles; she sits on the sofa and doesn't believe a word he's saying.

'And the children?' he says, chalking his cue again. It's such an easy way out to love children because one's own life has no meaning, and he talks about fathers who go along behind their sons saying very solemnly they're devoting their whole lives to them, and he laughs, almost angrily. Does simply handing it on give meaning to our life? Perhaps there are people whose lives are fulfilled and who have the right to call children; but to pass the time there is bowls and cards and a thousand entertaining professions and there is nothing more contemptible than to simply dump one's boredom onto one's offspring—

He puts the chalk back down again but doesn't continue his break.

It's just like a relay race, he laughs, a relay race with no finishing tape; they hand life over to us and say, 'Go on now, run with it, for twenty or seventy years.' And you run, you don't look at what you have in your hand, you just run and hand it on. And what, he says, if one of us asks what the aim of it is? You could be nasty and grab one of them by the sleeve and take him to one side and when he opens his hand—nothing. And that's what we're running for, one generation after another? It's nothing but a circus, round and round in a circle, with the dear Lord sitting in the middle perhaps, whipping us on with a hundred passions so the fun doesn't stop and He can laugh to His heart's content . . .

That's what he says.

When he thinks of all the things his parents did, out of boredom, and now you're supposed to go and do the same yourself and so on and so on . . .

They're not looking at each other, but Irene can sense that he's not laughing any more.

'What have the children done,' he asks after a while, 'to deserve having us wake them in the great nothingness and drag them out of the darkness, children who perhaps never wanted to enter life, children whose purpose it is to fill our emptiness until they are filled with despair at their own emptiness and in their turn go and call more children and so on and so on, born out of boredom, condemned to boredom, whole generations staring at you with questions in their eyes, with no idea what the point of their life is, and you who called them, you have the least idea of all . . .'

Then silence returns.

But Irene cannot believe that a person can think like that or that things are the way he makes out.

He smiles again. Oh yes, teaching is a marvellous profession, guiding children when you don't know the way yourself, telling them stories so they don't see the abyss . . .

He has picked up his cue again and aims at some ball chosen at random which just happens to be there on the green baize, so round and still and dead.

'I'm sure you'll be a good teacher.'

And she's not saying it as mockery, she believes it in all seriousness and, although she doesn't give any reasons and although he tells himself she can't know, he is stunned by her simple, quiet confidence; when he looks at her it is the first time there is no grimacing smile on his face.

Does she really believe that?

It's a pity that the clock should strike four as their conversation gradually becomes more reasonable; the coffee's brought in and and then her sister and brother-in-law come too.

When the time comes for introductions, it turns out that these two people, who have just been playing billiards together, don't even know each other's name and they have a laugh about it. And then he keeps being clumsy: either he misses the hand he's supposed to shake or he slips on his heavy, nailed climbing boots and almost knocks the little table over when they sit down to their coffee. And then a piece of cake breaks off his fork and falls on the floor. He becomes more and more confused, and when he remembers that two days ago these people saw him in the stream, standing in the water like a little boy playing with his boat of bark, he cannot get the idea out of his head that they are laughing at him, at his heavy climbing boots perhaps or at the way he holds his cup, and he's overcome with fear that he's going to crush the delicate cup and spill the coffee over their clothes and the fear is so strong that he can hardly follow what the people are saying to him so he just keeps nodding, whether or not it's appropriate . . .

Of course afterwards they want to watch them play, since Irene has told them how skilful he is, and while Irene now makes the most incredible shots, as a kind of proof of how much she's learnt from him, he naturally misses the simplest ones. At first he smiles, perhaps telling himself that it's only a game, and behaves as if it doesn't bother him, while with every miss he grows more and more tense; he starts to think he'll never hit a ball and eventually he doesn't say another word, even though the people are very friendly and, anyway, don't understand the game at all; when at last he does make a lucky cannon, they heap praise on him, at which he is offensively rude and says he can't play when people stand around gawping.

Such gaffes wouldn't be important if it wasn't that he'd made them hundreds of times . . .

At other times, for example, as a guest at a dinner party, he simply got up and left, or threw down a wine glass because he thought people were laughing at him and once, because he felt he was starting to stammer, he even abruptly slapped a professor who was smiling. There is scarcely any group where he's not behaved outrageously. He's aware of this and he's afraid, just as a sick person is afraid of another attack, and takes great care, until suddenly it's happened again. Except that previously you could say it was because you were young but soon this boorish behaviour will be all that's left of his youth.

Then, when they were alone again, they finished the game with hardly a word, and it was only when Irene, who had won easily, is putting her cue away in the rack that the silence is finally broken:

Why does he sometimes behave in such an odd manner? she asks, not reproachfully but in her usual open and natural way.

Then the two of them get the green cover, that has to be spread over the table, and leave everything as it should be.

She probably thinks he's crazy, he says, and once more he has his grimacing smile, once more the corners of his mouth are turned down in mocking contempt.

Of course not, she replies, very simply, as she smooths out the green cover again; when one gets to know him better she's sure he'll turn out to be a perfectly ordinary person.

*

He didn't even come down to dinner that evening and Irene waited—secretly waited—for him in vain when they were sitting in the lounge playing the cup-and-mouse game again. And late at night, when she's in her room, quite alone and taking off her bracelet, she can't get the odd fellow out of her mind and she still can't say what she might have done to offend him, what on earth can it be?

Then she puts her white shoes outside her door and when she hears a noise outside she goes to the stairs in her stocking-feet again, listening, but in vain.

Perhaps it's just curiosity she feels, or pity because she senses that he's making his life unhappier than it need be, some maternal feeling perhaps, that she ought to help him, quietly and with no visible gesture that might frighten him off, with no selfish motive, or perhaps there are other feelings involved—

She doesn't know.

For a long time she sits on the edge of the bed, undressing with slow, dreamy movements; at one point, just as she's about to put on her nightdress, she catches sight of her own bright image in the large mirror and her eye rests on it, with no false modesty, with natural pleasure even—and then with a slight start.

It's lovely when you're healthy and hard when you ought to be thinking of a sick man stuck in an armchair, whose hands are always moist when you come and who will never climb mountains again nor stand in foaming streams and lift heavy stones. And who wants to draw you down to him and kiss you, the way sick people kiss, all fearful and trembling, throwing a fit of jealously even when you're just playing with other people's children because you haven't any of your own, and full of suspicion of a healthy life, which he no longer has, and of her youth, which she has only once, one single time!

Sometimes everything's very hard, even for an Irene, whom no one would believe is sitting on the edge of the bed crying.

*

The next day, which is to be the last of her stay, it's still raining, a thin, delicate swishing noise, like an endless veil descending somewhere out of the greyness . . .

The walker, sitting on a tree stump up in the forest, is already wet through. He's holding a pine cone that is rotten and soft, and peeling off the scales, almost carefully, one by one.

Perhaps he's remembered that it's his birthday today. And that he's always said that anyone who hasn't achieved anything by the time they're thirty might as well go and hang themselves from the nearest tree . . .

Sometimes the hiss of the rain in the tall treetops gets louder and he watches the water running down the path and lets the drops trickle down his neck as well because he doesn't see the point of moving.

All he knows is that there's no way of rectifying it once you've made a mess of your life, there's no going back, no making up for lost time and putting things right, no mercy; he knows, more clearly than he's ever known, that everything you do or don't do, every mistake and every omission, is final and even just sitting here is something you can never go back to, that life always goes on, unstoppably, even if you don't see the point of moving.

Sometimes he holds his breath and it's as if you could hear time dripping from the trees, dripping away in single moments . . .

Otherwise there's nothing moving in the whole forest.

Maybe what you expect from your life is very presumptuous; it is very presumptuous that every creature thinks it must have meaning. In the end we're just a passage, vessels for a life that is happy with itself, sufficient unto itself. But perhaps there are some vessels that are empty—why should you not be honest with yourself when you're sitting all alone in a rain-soaked forest? Everything seems to empty to you. Sometimes you're enraptured by a landscape, by the colour of a passing cloud or a pond that happens to be glistening in the sun and you're glad, for the world is beautiful. You're happy and grateful simply to be alive in this world and it's enough that you can look at a flower and feel its stamens. Or sometimes a mushroom that you pick up and break apart can be very beautiful as well, or a piece of rotten wood you prise out of the tree stump and crush between your fingers. And sometimes you think that perhaps beauty is the point of the world, the point of our existence, that is perhaps what we are living for and that, too, is both true and false, like all the thoughts you pursue; you can peel them and crush them in your fingers and keep throwing them away. Like a pine cone or a mushroom or a piece of rotten wood that falls to pieces. And all that is left of the rapture nature bestows on us is the growing insight that you are far removed from this world that is beautiful and that perhaps has a meaning, you are banished from all natural completion, alone in your emptiness, alien and deaf in the great silence of a forest like this.

There is just the soundless mist swirling through the nearby trees, the trunks of which are wet and black, and in the distance, where you can make out the tall, frayed firs, they look like grey spectres standing somewhere on the steep slope, out of some bottomless, boundless nothingness—

Oh, it's not that he thinks you ought to be able to put it into words, the meaning of life, that you ought to be able to think it or even prove it! Given that everything that is true can only be believed. But the trouble is that he has so little belief in everything he does and it doesn't change anything however great an effort of will he makes.

It's a pity, but that's the way things are.

It is his will that will send him to the North Ridge, to the deed or to death, as he used to say, and that despite the fact that he is clear, clearer than ever, that he doesn't believe in the deed. Even if he should reach the summit, will that make him a different person? Still, what is left but ambition to someone who has no longing any more, no true longing?

It is already starting to get dark and he's still sitting on his tree stump. And shivering with the wet; but he feels as if he's still waiting, waiting for something in his heart.

No real longing and no real belief, and you can't even cry, as you did when you were a boy, there's no burning sensation in your chest, you don't feel you're going to be sick, and if you were to throw yourself to the ground, you'd would just be wet and ridiculous, for even pain is not enough any more, not even pain and you just sit there with your cold, empty despair . . .

With a heart that's died.

And a man like that, who has no firm ground under his own feet, is supposed to get married in ten days time and have a family and be a guide for others, a teacher, a father!

Then later, when it is already dark in the forest, all you can hear is single drops falling on the leaves and even the closest trunks abandon you; everything is submerged in the falling night and you're blind wherever you look.

*

Irene happens to be with the mountain guide when the dripping walker comes through the hall and goes up the stairs, without a word, without even a nod . . .

It is not difficult to guess what she's been talking to the guide about; the weather, of course, and then presumably the North Ridge, whether it really is as difficult as people say. The guide just smiles and doesn't even take his pipe out of his mouth. He could tell her a story that happened there two years ago; he picked up the pieces of two of his cousins on the upper Sand Glacier and their remains were buried together in one coffin because they couldn't tell which was which. But he just smiles and asks if she's thinking of doing the North Ridge? And when she just laughs, he says in a more serious tone that unfortunately they can't forbid people from attempting it but he's not bringing anyone down again, that's for sure. As he speaks, he knocks his pipe out, very thoroughly and calmly, before filling it and lighting it again.

Irene's pleasure at seeing the walker come back turns out to be premature. She does know that he's in the inn, but he stays out of sight and what she can't do is go and knock at his door . . .

Perhaps it would be a very beautiful and very happy night; perhaps he wouldn't even ask what she wanted and would just say he was expecting her or he was glad she'd come. Or they wouldn't say anything at all, just sit there together, with no questions or talk, which can only separate people. All he would know would be that she is leaving the next day and that they will never see each other again after that evening, and that knowledge would perhaps make their hearts freer than they had ever been, free of all the past, that weighs down on us, and free of all the future, that makes us hesitate, one evening that belonged entirely to the present, to their real existence, and if they were to kiss each other, they would know that it was their first and last kisses, and they would perhaps be kisses such as they had never known, words such as they had never heard, a happiness that was full of parting and can never become shallow, can never become blurred by repetition, one night, that only happened once, and perhaps for her, for Irene, it would be even more, even more than a significant memory, perhaps even the destiny to which she had been called.

But when she listens at his door and hears him moving about, she naturally hurries back as quickly and quietly as she can to her room; standing by her packed suitcases, her heart beating audibly for a long time.

But he doesn't come out—

He only stood up because he couldn't finish the letter he was trying to write to his fiancée, a very open and honest letter, he told himself when he began it, and a very inconsiderate one, he thinks when it's down on paper. Very inconsiderate and silly. What's the point of all this sentimental twaddle about not being able to get married because he's an empty shell and that it will be no disaster if he doesn't come back from the mountains and she finds herself another husband who can cope with life better, and that it is something he has to do for her sake . . .

What's the point of all that?

In the meantime the rain has stopped and it's very quiet outside, even the dripping in the tin gutter can no longer be heard.

He tore up the letter, but now he picks the pieces out of the waste-paper basket, places them on the outside window-ledge and sets light to them. And when he blows the ashes away, individual sparks flicker out into the darkness . . .

There are stars in the sky again, though not everywhere, and above the dark forest, that looks like a silhouette, the moon appears; at the moment the pale disc is ploughing its way through scudding clouds and sometimes it looks as if the moon is giving off silvery yellow puffs of smoke, then it is in the clear sky again, bright and still and cold.

Tomorrow will be a fine day.

Then he rings and asks for his bill and a bath—but make sure it's hot!—and packs his rucksack.

*

And, indeed, the next morning the sky is clear and blue again, as if it had just been washed; only the ground is still wet and the bushes glitter as if hung with pearls. And all the streams gurgle louder, in some places the water has even spilled onto the path and you have to watch your step amid all the shimmering rivulets running down the slope like molten sunlight. The hillside, that previously was nothing but dry scree and desiccated twigs, is now awash with water cascading merrily into the valley and on the high meadow, where your boots sink ankle-deep into soft brown mud, even the wooden water-wheel, which is usually full of spiders' webs, is running and turning a butter churn, clattering and throwing up a shower of drops that glisten in the early morning sun—

This is where Irene decides she will wait.

She set off first, an hour ago, while everyone in the inn was still asleep and there was no breakfast to be had, and now she's sitting in this alpine meadow, high above the valley, where you have a good view of almost the whole of the path as it winds its way up the slope . . .

How lonely the early morning is and the air feels as if no one had ever breathed; as if there were no creatures at all in the world, as if it still belonged to God alone.

She's sitting on a flat rock with her little rucksack on her knees and the simple slice of bread and butter, that is her breakfast, tastes wonderful, in fact she finds everything so marvellous that later she has to unpack the other things and look at them, just unpack and look at them of course, she tells herself. After all, you need to know what you have in your rucksack. There's a sausage, for example, and some cold roast meat, which she immediately stows away again, and the cheese has an attention-seeking smell, as if it wanted to be eaten that very moment. But you're not a child going out on a school trip who starts to eat the moment she's on the train; she just tosses a thin piece of the ham, which is already sliced, into her mouth, and she does it so quickly perhaps even God doesn't notice . . .

Meanwhile the first sunshine has also reached those down in the valley and the bell is just ringing for Mass in the little village below, where the brown chalets gather round the white church like a herd of animals; the bright, glassy sound floats up, very thin, delicate, constantly carried away by the wind.

There was no other way to the Oberhorn Hut, the guide said; and didn't she hear, last night when the walker was paying his bill and ordering his food, didn't she hear him say he was going to the Oberhorn Hut?

He'll come along, Irene said to herself, eating an egg—it was already a bit battered—then throwing the shell as far as she can down the slope. What more could she ask for: a cloudless morning and a soft-boiled egg, even with some salt to put on it—

It's great just to be alive!

Naturally they spot each other long before the solitary walker finally crosses the meadow and stands before her, so that neither shows any surprise; he just leans on his ice-axe to get his breath back and she's forced to blink as she turns to look at him. Where's he heading? she asks, and he looks back over the awakening valley as if he hasn't heard. He seems to have worked up a sweat already, even though he's only wearing a short-sleeved shirt, clearly his rucksack, tent and sleeping bag and the crampons and rope are weighing him down. Would he have anything against her accompanying him for a while? she asks, as if the idea has just occurred to her, and she doesn't give him much time to think about it before she has stood up and grasped her walking stick, full of enthusiasm for her own suggestion
. . .

After this high meadow there are no more clear paths, you're simply walking over open grassy slopes with huge boulders lying around; now and then there's a red arrow painted on them. It's very pleasant walking, for the ground is soft and almost springy, like a marsh, and their steps are silent. Just occasionally his ice-axe hits a stone and then there's a sharp clinking noise. Otherwise all you can hear is the ever-more distant and muted roar filling the valley bottom, the roar of all the streams and now and then a shrill whistle when a shy marmot takes flight.

She's never seen a marmot, she tells him, never in all her life; in fact she's never climbed a mountain, although she's always felt she'd like to—

He doesn't reply.

At one point later they pass through a hollow where there's still snow lying, almost to head height, but it's so grey and dirty you only realize it's snow when you step on it; it's where there was an avalanche and for a long time Irene feels a childlike joy, amazement, delight that she's tramped over snow, in the middle of summer!

And however taciturn and odd her companion is, she still enjoys this walk together, the cool morning air and the pathless meadows and the slow emergence of an unknown view the higher you get; she enjoys the way the mountain pines bend and twist, and the way the splintered trunks stand there after they've been struck by lightning; she enjoys it when they reach the last high meadow and rest by a wooden cross, when they gaze across the steep slopes shimmering with the blue-grey of the bilberries, across the ethereal haze of the valley to the sheer rocks that look as if they're coated in sugar . . .

It's just a thin layer of snow that will melt again at midday, he says, just so that he's at least said something.

Meanwhile the cattle are grazing all around and it's as if the tinkling of the cow bells is also part of the silence; there must be something like a hundred of them, calves and cows, and some have climbed as far as the first rocks; they stand there and gawp, then they swish their tails and go on browsing, while Irene's drinking her milk—

Then, when she still doesn't say anything about turning back and he waits in vain for her even to look back, he finally takes the stalk of grass out of his mouth and asks her straight out if she wants to go any farther?

Oh, she says, what is he thinking! She can keep on climbing like this for ages, for ten times as long, without getting tired.

He just watches the way her pale throat moves when she drinks and swallows, and the way the milk leaves a whitish shimmer on her blood-red lips every time.

Of course, she says, that's only if he's happy with that . . . ?

It would, of course, not be very polite of him to say he's not happy with that at all; that he plans to do things where another person would be in the way and that she should look for another guide if she really wants to go up into the mountains. But perhaps it's not the mountains she's interested in, perhaps she suspects what he has in mind and just wants to stop him. But he's not going to let himself be stopped, not for anyone, not even for some smiling woman, for it's finally time to follow your own resolve and not let yourself keep being distracted by your concern for others.

Unfortunately he hasn't time, he says, he has to get to the Oberhorn Hut by that evening.

She finishes her milk.

So how far is it to this Oberhorn Hut? she asks, and he, putting on a friendly expression, an expression of polite regret, has to explain to her clearly and in detail, that he's going to be away for three days and that of course without sufficient provisions she certainly can't—

But she has provisions, enough for three days; did he get cold roast meat and dried fruit as well, she asks, and a sausage like that? And ham? Though she's sure it's going to get dry, she says, as she tosses another slice into her mouth.

From the very first he has never quite believed that the meeting was pure chance; the only other possible objection occurs to him after a lengthy silence:

But what would her companions think if she simply stayed away for three days?

She just laughs, 'Oh, them!' and puts her little rucksack back on, already on her feet while he's still sitting:

Anyway, she'd already told them she was going with him, to the Oberhorn Hut.

Then she picks up her walking stick, all ready to go when he is . . .

*

It is to be assumed that those down in the inn will be making ironic remarks when the two of them don't appear for lunch and miss dinner as well, and they'll be smiling, not maliciously, but with that covert gloating people always have when a love affair starts; there is a secret comfort in knowing that everyone must take this ordinary route, even if they come along with crampons and pitons . . .

But another guest has arrived, a young lady who at the moment is sitting at the little table where the odd fellow used to sit. Like every new guest, she looks a bit lost and embarrassed. She also seems to be very young, twenty or twenty-one perhaps. She pulls her bread to pieces, eating two whole slices by the time the soup comes. And when someone asks her if she would like some wine, she gives a slight start and then just shakes her head, very hastily; then she blushes and just stares at her plate until the fruit has been eaten and she's the first to stand up and leave, quickly and quietly; they all somehow feels sorry for her, even though no one knows who she is . . .

Outside it's a mild evening, as is right and proper after after a fine day, an evening with large, smouldering clouds passing over the mountains, and you feel it's nice to sit outside the hut for a while, to lean against the warm wall with your feet up on a railing and perhaps smoke a pipe, to be silent and feel the glow of the late-evening sun on your face and arms as you look out over the darkening valleys, over the nearby glaciers and the constantly changing clouds—

The hut warden says the clouds aren't bad and since you look at him with a doubtful expression he even promises a clear night, with stars even.

Then he goes on smoking.

He seems to be a decent chap and he's certainly pleased someone has come, even a woman. The first this year, as he says. Otherwise he stays silent, just standing beside the stranger and looking out, as she is, and answering when he's asked a question, and when there are no more questions, he still stands there and isn't bothered by the silence, until it's time to light the stove and put the soup on . . .

Then they're alone, Irene and the walker, outside the hut.

They're still watching the mist boiling up from the valleys. Sometimes it shimmers like red copper and it's as if everything is dissolving in a haze, as if the mountains are floating and merging with the passing clouds. There are moments when you hardly know what's the earth and what the sky. Until somewhere a hole opens up and you can see a deep valley, deeper and darker than you would have thought, and spectral shadows gliding over the corpse-like pallor of the glaciers. Ridges emerge too, like steel-blue saws. Thus it changes with every breath you take, this brightness hanging in the air. And the distant murmur of countless glacier streams somewhere down below. You feel like spreading your arms, leaping off the cliff and flying through space, floating as if in a dream and melting like shining mist . . .

What is the purpose of our life?

It is Irene who comes back to their conversation; she has her hands clasped round her right knee and is leaning her head back against the warm wall.

Do we have to know that? she asks, slightly uncertainly and very innocently . . .

She's never known, she says after a while she has clearly spent thinking about it. She's just got on with life. Sometimes sad, sometimes happy, the way life is. When she goes out riding, she's always happy; then she even sings, despite the fact that she hasn't got a voice. And she always enjoys swimming, and she talks at length about the sea and about sailing. But she's happiest of all, she says later, she's happiest of all with little children; though she likes having a nice dog around, they used to have a black Alsatian at home until the poor thing was run over, and the suffering the animal went through and the look in its eyes made her very sad; it's bowels had been all ripped out, isn't that terrible?

He nods.

Though, she says, he mustn't think there aren't other things she's been through—

At that she stops, very abruptly, in a way that makes him look up; he still can't say how old he thinks she is, it's very difficult when she just sits there, looking down at the ground, sometimes she's an absolute child, but then there's that twist of the lips when she's not speaking . . .

But on the whole, she says after a while, she thinks she enjoys being alive, though she's never thought about it before.

Then she looks at him:

Does he know what the purpose of our life is? she asks and doesn't seem devastated when he confesses that he doesn't know either, although he has thought about it; she just smiles:

'But look—you're alive as well.'

If you can call it being alive! he says with a scornful laugh, knocking his pipe out on the wall.

Sometimes, he says, he thinks life must be something that is greater, unutterably greater than everything he's ever experienced, and that is perhaps the only hope that keeps you alive: that you perhaps don't know life yet, just its name.

Irene watches him as he takes his pipe apart, more to play with it than to clean it.

You can't even know, he says, whether you've ever once been happy in your life. When he was young, he often thought: This is happiness. But when he looks back, he says, when he puts everything together he called happiness at some time or other, and when he considers that it's the harvest of three decades, of half a life, of all the years of his youth—

Then he just smiles. It would be very sad if that were happiness, the happiness of which we talk so often, for which we put up with so many other things, so many ugly and ordinary things, above all so many ridiculous things, so much mundane routine.

Outside the mist is still rising from the darkening valleys and there are moments when you just seem to be sitting on a reef in the middle of a slowly undulating sea of cloud breaking on the glowing rocks with silent spray.

He doesn't think, he says—and perhaps he doesn't even know he's saying it and to whom he's saying it— he doesn't think he's lived up to now.

Irene remains silent.

There are seeds that never sprout and never bloom, he goes on, and nature is so great and so profligate, who can say how many people it tries out before it gets one who is really alive and who knows to the limit what it is when they talk about life, about pain, about longing and work and happiness? He himself doesn't know anything about all that; only in dreams you sometimes sense how boundless those words are that we all misuse for our experiences, and how little, how ridiculously little you make of what you call your life. And which is nothing other, he says, than a series of wasted days, which are always less than what you had planned for them; weeks and years pass without you realizing, often you think it's all just one single day, one long everyday which is always the same: getting undressed and cleaning your teeth, just as you did yesterday and

have done for years, then sitting on the side of the bed
for a while and winding up the alarm clock again, slowly
and with the indisputable realization that once again
you've achieved nothing, just as you did yesterday, as
you have done for years. In the end you won't have
lived at all, not even for the time it takes for a single
breath, not for a single breath, as is appropriate for an
agonising birth or the horror of a solitary death . . .

Then he laughs:

Or does she call it life, he asks, when you watch
your beard and your fingernails grow?

But Irene still remains silent.

She has been watching the sun sink, the mist lose its
glow; it's getting darker with every moment, from time to
time a star seeps through, somewhere between floating
clouds which are now pale and whitish once more . . .

There are presumably others who feel that way, she
says: that you sometimes feel very superfluous because
you're not there for anyone else, just for yourself, and
because that really isn't enough; and that you sit on the
side of the bed in the evening, horrified at how quickly
your youth has been squandered and how little happiness you have been granted or have brought about.
There are perhaps others who feel like that, she says,
and she probably means it as a comfort when she says
it's the way ordinary life is.

He's holding his empty pipe, which is still slightly
warm, in his fist and looking out over the balustrade

just in front of him to where nothing can be distinguished any more.

Ordinary life . . .

He just says, 'No!' and shakes his head—that's the problem, in that case he'd rather not live, not like that, not as an ordinary person, never!

Then it gets darker and darker. They can't see each other's face and they're glad. Even Irene, who would like to ask him whether he doesn't know what love is? Perhaps she's just a heartbeat away from saying the question out loud—

But then the warden taps on the window from inside:

The soup's ready.

And when they stand up, without a word and shivering a little, Irene once more gets childish pleasure out of the clatter the heavy wooden clogs they're wearing for the hut make on the floor. In fact, as soon as they're back in the light she seems very merry and carefree, positively high spirited, the way she's always seemed to him so far, a way that doesn't go with the voice he heard out in the darkness just now. When they're in the hut she even dances to make the clatter of the wooden clogs louder and the warden grins all over his bearded face as he pours the steaming soup and scatters the hot pieces of smoked bacon fat over it with a spoon.

And when should he wake them in the morning? he asks later, when they've finished eating and he's

washing the blue-and-white dishes; and are they planning something big? Everything depends on the
weather, is the walker's rather curt reply as he leafs
through the visitors' book; but then he feels he has to
add that he intends going up to the Ochsenjoch and he
eventually tells him he has a tent and is going to camp
out for the night there on the col. As he speaks, he continues to leaf through the visitors' book and the warden,
who smokes his pungent pipe even while he's drying
the dishes, realizes the stranger is unwilling to talk
about his intentions; so he doesn't ask any more questions but silently puts the crockery back in the little cup-
board and just says it can be very cold, a night at that
altitude when you've only got a tent.

Then he puts another log in the stove; it seems that
he intends to make another pot of tea before they go to
bed. At least there's water simmering in a copper pan.
Otherwise all that can be heard for a long time is the
ticking of the clock . . .

They once spent the night up on the Ochsenjoch,
he tells them after he's joined them at their table. Also
in a tent. It was two years ago, when they had to go and
search for the two men who hadn't come back from the
North Ridge, he says, sucking on his pipe between
words, and that had been a very cold night.

And once more all that can be heard is the crackle
of the stove when the fire collapses, and the bubbling of
the water that is gradually coming to the boil.

And Irene, who had perhaps hoped she could persuade him to abandon his reckless plan, hardly says a word the whole evening . . .

Later, after they have sipped the hot tea, slowly, with both hands around the mug, and when they go outside again, the mist really has fallen away and it's a clear, starry night. Just the valley is like a black hole at their feet. But the mountains look as if they're made of glass and everything has a pale, hard brightness without it being obvious from where it is coming. Perhaps from the Milky Way shimmering over the frozen snows. And over all is a silence which secretly makes their hearts pound the longer they look, a silence which gives you the feeling that it would kill you if you could really hear it.

Then, almost without realizing it, they put their arms round each other's shoulder, since it's so cold outside, and they just smile, when at one point they look at each other, not in embarrassment at all, just a little surprised . . .

Has he already been in love with a woman? Irene is already asking him that same evening; or does he perhaps not know what love is? Because he'd said he didn't know what happiness was.

But he just laughs:

Oh, yes, love is when you get engaged and wear a ring—

But she's serious, she's not interested in his jokes, and it's no help to him that it actually is very cold outside, that his teeth are already chattering, and hers too; she won't go in until she's had her answer.

Let's assume, he says after a while, she was in love with someone, for example she knew she could never forget him if she left him and she wouldn't leave him anyway because she can't stand having a guilty conscience, or above all because she can't imagine loving another person even more, as much, perhaps, but not more—would she call that love?

Irene doesn't answer.

When he was a boy, he tells her, in high spirits now, he was always outraged when a decent man could marry again after his first wife had died; in his opinion, such a man ought not to survive, if he really had loved his wife—

Oh?

But now he's the one who is serious when, after a moment's reflection, he adds: He thinks he would survive.

It's difficult for Irene, who would like to give him an answer, a good answer that would overcome his bad thoughts; for it is not acceptable to a woman, especially a young woman, for doubt to be cast on love, which is her vocation. She always feels as if she has to fight for the honour of all loving hearts, and even if she knows, knows from her very own experience, how dark a heart can be, even her own heart, she would still like to say how good and wonderful love is, how great and pure, how happy, and that he should always follow his heart if it longs for love . . .

But it's difficult when he replies to that too with his unshakeable scepticism: how can you tell whether a longing really comes from the heart? And there are also hearts which have never known love, just the need for infidelity . . .

Back in the hut, on the wooden sleeping platforms, he shows her how to swathe yourself in blankets. He wraps her up like a mummy and when she stands there, tightly sheathed, he picks her up in his strong arms and lays her down; and she gets another blanket over her feet, to make sure she won't feel cold. She watches him without a word as he sees to all that with almost fatherly concern, then he takes the lamp from the nail, stands up and holds out his hand to her. When she looks at him, the flickering candle is reflected in her big eyes, right at the back:

Does he still wonder why she waited for him, this morning, she asks, and why she wanted to come with him?

She smiles and doesn't let go of his hand. She's close to telling him everything, so that he won't get the wrong idea about her . . .

Why?

Should she tell him?

But then she feels ashamed and just makes a joke of it:

Because she wanted a free guide, that's why she came with him! And once more they wish each other good night.

Then it's silent in the hut.

*

And so Barbara, the young woman on the inn below, has waited the whole evening in vain. There are fewer and steps on the stairs; all that can be heard is the boy collecting the shoes put outside the doors and then there's no sound of the last of the staff any more. And when the waiting woman does prick up her ears again and hold her breath, it's only a guest up late.

With a young lady! the friendly landlord told her and she just managed to keep herself under control until she was back in her room and had locked the door . . .

Since then she has sat there staring at the walls, but they can't explain either why a man who is loved simply goes off two weeks before the wedding, manifesting such an urge for freedom. It's the room he was in the previous day; now her suitcase, which is still unopened, is on the wobbly table where he wrote to her, and perhaps it's even the same alpine roses in the old-fashioned jug. And perhaps even the same pillows, into which he pressed his face with its look of despair. But things are mute and don't reveal what they know, nor can you see the thoughts that have been thought in a room, thoughts about a manly deed or manly unfaithfulness.

*

It is still early the next morning and the two others, who left the Oberhorn Hut at first light, are already sitting on the top of a mountain; it is still early and really glorious at that time, when no mist has yet risen from the valley and everything is so fresh and shining, the glaciers and the peaks couldn't be more white, more pure, and the air is like glass, so bright and cold, even though you can already feel the warmth of the sun.

Irene is lying on her back, her hands clasped behind her head, like someone dreaming . . .

What she still finds most amazing is perhaps not even this view but the simple fact that he has taken her up a mountain at all, even though he said yesterday that he didn't have the time, and even though she didn't ask again.

In fact, it's as if he's a different man . . .

He whistles as he pours the tea or opens a tin; he seems content and cheerful as never before. He points out the mountains, he knows them all, and names the Matterhorn, the Weisshorn, the Dom, and even, in the pale glassy distance, the Finsteraarhorn and the Eiger;

as he does so his head at times comes very close to hers, so that she can look along the finger he's pointing. He also shows her the tracks winding over the dazzling snow-slope, which are their own tracks and then, when they've eaten and drunk, he puts everything back in his sack and gives it her to rest her head on, so that she can be more comfortable, he says . . .

Sometimes there's a keen wind, as there usually is on top of a mountain, and long banners, that glitter like silver in the sun and then veil over again, stream from the white ridges soaring up into the blue sky.

Irene can't know why he's so different, so natural, for the first time, and so content with this delightful world, which is lying at their feet, so to speak, and which he keeps looking at, for long periods, without that guarded expression, with a serene, healthy expression. Nor why he looks at her now and then, simply looks at her lying beside him, already brown, at the way the wind plays with her hair, or the way her breast keeps rising and falling and rising as she breathes, and the way she's enjoying the sun with her eyes closed, or occasionally blinking, with her lips slightly parted and some kind of happy smile on them.

Perhaps it reminds him of the woman who appeared in his dream, a woman who wasn't Barbara and wasn't Irene, but both and neither and all women, as is possible in dreams, a woman who has a hundred faces and whom you can't escape, since she's there in all women, and who opened her arms, a woman so maternal and at the same time so different, as is possible in dreams, so indescribably simple . . .

And how quiet it is when you look up again, here on the summit, how quiet and lonely. There is just a black chough there that sits on the white cross until it hops into the void and spreads its black wings to break its plunge; then it sails round the cliffs in soundless loops, carried by the wind and floating away over depths that make humans dizzy, almost without flapping its wings at all. And then, when this last living creature has disappeared, there is just your own breath you can hear, or a rustling sound when the wind plays with a piece of paper the bread was wrapped in or a mug that's fallen over.

Irene, still lying on her back, didn't open her eyes when she felt him close by her, when he kissed her, on her lips and forehead and eyes—

Later she says, with a smile:

Hasn't he known for ages that she's in love with him?

And, for the first time, his face is without doubt, without fear and without mockery. And without ambition. A smiling face that shows how happy he is, how perfectly happy, even if later he might once more claim he doesn't know what happiness is.

'Oh, yes,' he says, nothing more, and lies down on his back as well, clasps his hands behind his head and stares into the blue distance:

It would be heavenly, he says, if they never had to go back down to the valley ever again, never ever again
. . .

On a mountain top there's nothing to disturb your happiness, there is just this unbounded silence, and it's good to lie on your back with your eyes closed and the glow of the sun through your lids, red and blue and yellow, like a colourful church window. Or like a meadow in bloom. Or sometimes like merry lanterns, all swaying haphazardly and reflected in a pool. The things you can see when you close your eyes and watch the blood in your eyelids! Ships sailing on golden seas and coasts emerging in the glittering distance, foreign coasts with towers and white birds circling round the towers and over the silvery spindrift. And you can see flowers, nothing but flowers, which perhaps signify kisses or tears or ecstasy or death, a blood-bright bouquet, a shimmering bouquet, and shining ribbons and girls dancing, you can see the notes they're singing, and everything is colour, everything is in a whirl; there's no standing still and no emptiness, there's adventure, there's the blaze of passionate hearts which are not suffocating in grey ash but afire with love, hate, joy and sorrow, in all the colours that are there in your blood and that float past and want to be lived out . . .

At one point, quite unexpectedly, he asks her:

Would she go with him? Simply go away, leave everything behind?

She has to blink as she turns her head to look at him . . .

To some country, he says, where there's no humdrum daily round, where they don't know anyone, where they could really live, without ties and without having to make allowances, without anything that's not part of it, a real life, a life not stuck in a rut but open to experience, a life we know from our longings, a new, a different life, a life worth living—!

Irene remains silent; but she feels as if she's already thought that herself.

Why do we not follow our longing? Why is it? Why do we bind and gag it every day, when we know that it's truer and finer than all the things that are stopping us, the things people call morality and virtue and fidelity and which are not life, simply not life, not a life that's true, great, worth living! Why don't we shake them off? Why don't we live when we know we're here just this one time, just one single, unrepeatable time in this unutterably magnificent world?

There's so much you could do, he says, if you have the courage. You could get everything you possess together and sell it all; you'd have enough money to get across the frontier and through the neighbouring country. It would probably be best, he said, if you headed south. You could hike and sleep in villages whose names you'd never heard of; they'd come to designate secret and unique nights. And in the summer you could sleep out in the open, in a field somewhere where a foreign moon floats over the white mist and foreign birds call. You could go to farmers, whose language you don't understand, and bind sheaves, for a whole day, just to keep body and soul together, and it wouldn't be an easy life, he admits, it would be a hard, often a desperate, life, a gruelling life with no firm ground under your feet, but it would be a life! And it could be that at some point you might find a place where the other has to go on and there would be farewells, perhaps for ever, farewells in foreign towns where bright ships lie in the harbour, where you kiss and cry and don't worry about the faces you don't know, and where you simply sit on a suitcase, alone, with no ties and no address and ready to go with any wind that blows. And it could be that you might meet a pale man on the ship and that you were fortunate, that you might get on a farm where you'd stay for many years doing useful work. It could just as well be that you founder at sea and recognize some god or other before you go under, a real god perhaps, who redeems us when he lets us die. Why should it not happen? The possibilities of our life are like the winds, so why do we never dare to set our sails? Anything is better than a life that is not lived—pain and despair and crime, they're all better than emptiness! And it could be that you stay true to each other because you made no promises, that you meet once again, somewhere in the world, one evening perhaps, you could say the names of those villages to each other, the names designating secret and unique nights, you could tell each other what has happened since and that would certainly be no small matter, there would be a lot of torments and mistakes, but no emptiness, it would be an evening to make everything good again, an evening worthy of our birth and our death, it would perhaps be in a station, with people rushing past like noisy shadows, or on an embankment where you look out over the sea and hear the endless roar, where you can't speak, only hold hands. How great could such a love be that refused to hold on! And one morning, when the other is still asleep, why should you not quietly set off, why should you not leave happiness before it leaves you, why should you stifle every longing? Living is longing, and it could be that what was lost is greater than everything you grasped, and that you only really live when you have the courage to lose things, when you throw off everything, your name and your citizenship and everything, just not your destiny, when you live as if every day were your last day—

Then for a long time they stare up into the blue sky, into a blueness that seems so deep, when you're lying on your back looking at nothing else, so deep and dark, as if you could see, beyond the day, the cosmic night.

Courage, he says, it just takes courage—

And when he sits up and looks at her there is a seriousness in his face, a fervent, youthful seriousness, she hardly expects:

Does she have that courage? he asks, holding her tight, almost painfully tight. Does she have the courage to set off on a new and real life in which you don't have to make allowances and in which you risk everything for your longing? And really set off? And set off with him?

'Oh!' is all she says . . .

Then she pulls him down, with a soft, gentle power, right into her arms, right onto her breast and with kisses that are very hot and very unbridled they make the promise: that they are going to forget everything, forget everything that is past and sacrifice everything that is not part of their future, of their longing, of their love, of their new life.

'Everything?' she asks.

And he swears to it:

'Everything!'

*

During the whole day Barbara hardly left the inn at all, or at least only went to places where she could still see the ways in; and when, finally, evening is approaching, she takes a deck chair and sits on the grassy terrace immediately in front of the building, so that he will have to go right past her when he comes home with the other woman.

The air that evening is like silk, the sky is still cloudless so that you could believe the distant mountains were painted on the sky, they seem so insubstantial, so delicate, so gossamery . . .

It is, moreover, strange how sure Barbara is that she knows what kind of person this other woman must be. Although no one has said a word about her, she knows, for example, that she's over twenty-one. She simply knows. Perhaps she's already married, or has been married, even if she naturally doesn't tell him. At least she's not a girl any more, and that's what a girl fears most of all. A girl is so shy when she's in love, the man only has to say he has a headache for a girl to stop talking, she believes every word he says, a girl is happy to be led, or at least that's how it appears, for she believes in the man she loves, just as she used to believe in her father and even before that perhaps in God, she believes in everything he does, she believes in his strength, in his future, in his talents, and if he's occasionally in despair, then she's sad but still convinced he's a great, an incomparable, man, true she never understands his ambition but she takes it seriously and never doubts it. And perhaps that is exactly what sometimes exasperates a man? Especially if he doesn't believe in himself any more. A woman can never understand his ambition either, but then she doesn't take it seriously, she accepts everything he thinks and everything he talks about in the same way as she accepts the cut of his suits, and when he talks and talks, about God and the world, she nods and shows him her legs, and perhaps, Barbara thinks, men like that better than when you think hard and then always agree. Men do like to shape the creatures they love, you can see it already in boys: when they've moulded something according to what they have in mind, they throw it away, it no longer has any attraction, any value for them. So perhaps it wasn't a good thing that you said everything the man you love did and said was good, yes, for the first time, on this evening and outside this inn, Barbara suspects that the things a man you love does can be very bad, and she suspects it with a certain pride, for it is perhaps the first step on Barbara's gradual road to becoming a woman

As long as it's not already too late.

At this time the tent is being put up on the Ochsenjoch, the col at the foot of the North Ridge; the pegs are pushed into the hard, stony ground and then, after they've spread out the white canvas, he inserts the poles and Irene is delighted to see that now it's a proper tent and you can look in, as if it's a little room, just big enough for two people.

They are in a joyous mood.

Coming down from the summit they found some edelweiss, the first edelweiss Irene's picked with her own hands, and they slid down long snow slopes, whizzing down with cries of delight, and afterwards, when they were at the bottom, getting their breath back and looking where they'd come from, arm in arm, they can hardly believe they've been on that summit and it was all like looking up when you're drunk.

And now it's still a fine, warm evening, with hardly any wind at all; the lower Sand Glacier is already in shadow, as is the nearby, immense North Ridge, which the walker is not bothered about any more . . .

But here, where the two are sitting, the sun is still shining. She watches the way he does everything, the way he fishes the stove out of his rucksack and assembles it, the way he goes to the nearby stream, clambering over the sharp rocks to find the best place and the cleanest water; the way he pours it out then refills the pan and comes back very carefully with the full container. Most of all she would like to give him a kiss, at this precise moment, and she would like to hold him tight so that he would feel how grateful she is, how glad, how happy!

What's all this? he asks

What indeed is all this . . .

He's used stones to make a hearth sheltered from the wind so they won't have to wait too long for the water to boil. Then he pours in the paraffin, screws the top back on the bottle and puts it away. He does it all very calmly, contentedly, without a word.

Now the deep and distant valleys are filled with blue haze again and the evening light over the heights is growing thinner, milder and more golden; it's as if everything facing west suddenly has a face, every rock and every blade of grass, everything is glowing, as if it were praying to the setting sun, and everything now has a sharp shadow close behind it, every rock and every blade of grass and every pan . . .

Once more she breaks the silence, just as he's about to light the stove:

'Are you married?'

She has taken hold of his hand and looks at the ring, which is very slim, and then at him, and he feels sorry that for a moment it's as if her exultant joy has been driven away.

He's engaged—yes.

Then he has to strike another match. When the wick is burning, he puts the lid on the water and just says:

Didn't she know that already?

She looks at the thin, bluish, almost invisible flame on the stove and he takes a tin out of his rucksack that gives off a smell of coffee when he opens it.

Does his fiancée know where he is this evening? she asks, or has he lied to her?

He places the coffee beside the stove so that everything will be to hand when it boils; he doesn't forget the sugar either.

It wouldn't be the first time, he says offhandedly.

Then they finally hear the rattle of the pan lid. But it's not boiling yet. There are just those tiny bubbles forming, like pearls on the pan, and he puts the warm lid back on. And says, without looking at her:

Did she not think he was capable of it?

What? Of getting engaged?

Of lying . . .

When he looks at her, Irene is still sitting in the same posture, resting her body on her left elbow, chewing a little blade of grass.

She presumes everyone lies, she says.

Then they drink their coffee, which is very hot. And they're still sitting outside after the sun has gone down and the mountains are growing pale. It's as if these mountains, which for an hour seemed fused to the glowing sky and no more than a gleam floating in the air, return to their real density; they are hard and grey, while the sky now has a glassy brightness and rises, higher and higher, until the first stars seep through in the east.

They didn't say anything else, or at least only things to do with the coffee or the dishes or clearing away.

It is not until late, when their shivering gradually becomes audible, that they decide it's time to get into the tent at last. They take off their boots and stuff them with dry paper, as you're supposed to. They've taken their two rucksacks in as well so they won't be soaked through in the morning. Everything is stowed away in the cramped space. The torch is given one last check and then hung up in an accessible spot before they crawl into the sleeping bag and make themselves comfortable . . .

But they haven't put the awning down yet—it also serves as the door—so they can look out for a while longer from the snug warmth of the tent.

So now they're lying together, in their tent that seems to get whiter and whiter the darker the night becomes. Sometimes a kind of shiver runs across the canvas. Then it's still and taut once more, in the shape of a large coffin, and all they can hear is the murmur of an invisible stream from the glacier plunging over a rock somewhere, an endless, cold murmuring.

He once vowed to himself that he would be an exception, he tells her in almost cheerful tones. That he wanted to be a person who never lied. Though that was a long time ago. It was perhaps the first time he had been alone with a girl, also in the mountains and there was no special reason why he should make the vow. They intended to tell each other everything, whatever should happen between them, and for the whole summer it was like a game, admitting every harmless truth. They were both still very young. And once, while they were walking through the woods together, the girl tore her good skirt and then he demanded that she simply tell her parents, who knew nothing of their friendship, the plain truth. That was always best, he said. And she did tell them and the same week her parents sent her off to the French-speaking part of Switzerland to learn the language. That's what you get with your truth, she wrote in her first letter; at the time, however, he remained firm and adamant and fully convinced that complete happiness could only come with complete truth, anything else would only defile their love, he wrote to her. And there was definitely something of genuine belief in that. Of course, not everything was that simple, since there were also truths that were not harmless. Once, after a party, he had to accompany a woman late at night, a stranger, an adult woman, and they walked arm in arm. Everything had happened so suddenly, on that mild, sultry summer's night, and there had been kisses such as he had never known before, adult kisses, wilder and hotter, overpowering for a young person, it was a new and such a different world this woman was was offering him, a new kind of love which wasn't satisfied with dreams, which believed in fulfilment—

When he realizes he has started reminiscing, he falls silent for a while; it must be the first time he has told anyone else at all about that.

'And what about truth?' he asks her. Does she think it's always best to tell the plain, unvarnished truth?

But Irene doesn't reply . . .

Yes, he says later with a smile, you grow older, that's all, more mature, so to speak, or at least you conform to the outside world and presumably part of that is to sacrifice one's own clear conscience rather than someone else's good opinion, which would perhaps be easier; things are not as simple as you thought when you were still young.

Gradually a damp chill spreads over the ground, but they still don't close the tent . . .

Perhaps he goes on reminiscing, since he remains silent all the time, and thinking how everything turned out so differently, even that difference you once vowed and believed in, believed in so passionately when you were still young. You couldn't understand adults, who accepted that kind of love, and you were horrified to think that you yourself were the child of that kind of love, that you couldn't exclude your own parents from your general revulsion. You could only vow that you would never be part of it yourself. And there was nothing that made the young person you were more outraged than when adults said you would get used to everything, the same had happened to them. Was it meant to be a comfort that they too had succumbed to this world? And it was out of defiance that you were determined to show them you were different, and all the generations who had followed this path before us were not sufficient as a warning; you were young enough to despise them all, the whole of humanity, you refused to be dictated to by thousands of years of history and you didn't hesitate to weigh yourself in the balance against a whole world and see yourself as equal in weight to all of them and as a saint, different from everyone who had ever lived! And then the moment came that proved all that wrong. Perhaps you could still have refused to accept it, as you had done so often before. But there came a point when you hadn't refused to accept it, though perhaps you only realized afterwards; it had all been like a big, if inadvertent, mistake, but it had happened and when you came out of the woods that night, the stars were still twinkling as ever and nothing had changed, nothing had collapsed and nothing had risen over the woods, which remained dark and silent behind you. You weren't even devastated, not shattered like a precious vessel that has fallen on the ground, nor the opposite, you weren't redeemed. Just sad, as you have basically been ever since, and now your delusion of being different was burnt out. You reached the first street lamp and people walked past as if nothing had happened, and the buildings just stared straight in front of them, simply straight in front, as if they'd known it all for ages. And from then on the world seemed to have no mystery and you didn't really know what to say. You still walked together, arm in arm, and perhaps one of you said, it's getting late, or, it's going to rain tomorrow. And that was what you had been yearning for to the very depths of your being, that? Somewhere you said good night to each other, with a very vague and absentminded smile, not embarrassed, but like two people who realized they had been mistaken and that it couldn't be changed, and it was only when you were back home, when you were alone, that everything unravelled and you cried perhaps, like the child you no longer were. You felt you were very old, all at once very old, and if death were to come you couldn't even say any more: Dear Death, I haven't lived yet. Nor show that your hands were clean any more—

He can't stop himself thinking of all this, now, while he's lying in his tent with the young foreign woman; he just smiles occasionally, so she won't think he's forgotten her, or he puts his arm round her thin shoulders when she shivers.

Outside there is no light visible that has been lit by human hand. There are just the stars glittering above the mountains and it's bright, so that you can even see the blades of grass on the ground nearby, almost as bright as day, though it's a different gleam, a lifeless gleam pouring over things, dull and without shadow, very strange, as if one were on another planet where there's no life, on a planet which, with all its rocks and ice, is not made for man, however indescribably beautiful it may be.

'Oh, yes!' Irene says at some point, presumably meaning that she's guessed his silent thoughts.

He mustn't think he's the only person going round with a guilty conscience, she says—

Maybe he smiles now, the way people smile when they are in love or preoccupied, or he strokes her hair, since it has a very unreal shine in this starlight night.

She too, she says, wouldn't have believed herself capable of it. And then she keeps plucking at one of the guy ropes as she tells him about her husband, who spends his days in an easy chair and always has moist hands when you come, and whose eyes she fears as nothing else in the world, as she fears only death, and perhaps it's very cowardly and mean of her, but she can't do anything about it, she can't love a sick man, she says. When she's away, she always thinks she ought to be able to, but when she sees him again and takes his moist hands—you can't love a dying man, she says, you can't do that!

He remains silent.

Can he not understand that? she asks, almost vehemently, at least very anxiously.

He just didn't know she was married, he replies in soothing tones . . .

Oh, she says later, he mustn't think she's never loved her husband, really loved him, and she tells him how they met, it was in a seaside resort, how they went sailing together and then he had to go abroad and they wrote to each other, almost every day, really. And how she was overjoyed when he finally found a job and they could get married, she was twenty at the time and she also tells him how they lived together in their marriage, which lasted five years, and what a good, cheerful and

successful man he had been. Until he had the accident
with the car and they thought everything was fine, she
says, he'd gone back to work. And then the problem
with his lungs had appeared, and she speaks more and
more slowly and with lengthy pauses, and it's been like
that for three years now.

Then both remain silent . . .

'A divorce?' she says, shrugging her shoulders: he
doesn't want one, no sick man wants to divorce himself
from life, and no healthy woman, she adds, wants to
have sick children—!

Their faces, close to each other, look as if they're
made of wax they're so bright, and they can also watch
each other breathe, watch the grey breath disappear in
the great, dark night.

Now he knows why she's come with him, she says,
and presumably now he feels sorry for her . . . ?

It sounded very bitter and he knows that anything
he might say would be very stupid. She's lying beside
him and he looks at her for a long time, without being
able to make out her face, which is in the darkness now.
And when she feels him lean towards her to kiss her, she
takes his head in both her hands and holds him back,
very gently and very firmly:

Don't—

And then, when his wandering hand touches her
face he knows she's silently crying.

Everything is so ridiculous, this whole life, even if you are brave enough to take risks, hopelessly ridiculous and ordinary . . .

He didn't say another word.

Then she took his hand, but he doesn't hold hers. All she can hear is the murmur of the stream, which keeps her awake, hour after hour, but she can't tell from his hand whether he's asleep or dreaming or also awake. It's like a dead man's hand she's holding, softly yet firmly, and she doesn't want to let go, not until morning.

*

However, when Irene wakes up next morning, because her back is cold or because the brightness is already coming through the damp canvas, she finds she's alone. There's no one outside either, of course. The white tent stands solitary among the grey boulders, wet and slack, and all that remains is the endless murmur of the stream.

It's no use remembering that she intended to keep hold of his hand, that she shouldn't have fallen asleep; remembering and blaming herself doesn't make any difference whatsoever, nor does the sob she finally gives, out loud, like a lost child, when she realizes where he's gone . . .

It's not even four o'clock and everything's still grey, the glacier and the moraines and the cliffs, wholly grey beneath this empty, colourless sky which has lost all its stars.

Later she called out, of course, as loud as she could and ever more despairingly, until eventually she does actually hear his voice, but very distant and thin and fragile. Beyond the glacier, and she can't understand what he's shouting, even if she holds her breath. He must be very high up already. Now and then a sharp, metallic sound can be heard when his ice-axe hits the rocks; but she can't see him, when she spots something it's always a rock that doesn't move, and she doesn't even know how big a person will look at that distance . . .

Then the first peaks start to take on colour, at first like bronze, then like copper and finally even like gold. And the snow-covered summits, which get the first light, are like ivory. And you can see the grey shadows slowly sinking; the daylight reaches lower and lower levels and the rocks, that are now bathed in sunlight, are once more as pale as bones. Later the top edge of the glacier shines, as if it were nickel-plated, and then it's as if the side were melting in a blaze of white-heat, you can't look any more as the sunlight is just starting to pour over the ridge.

But Irene is still sitting on the stone they sat on yesterday evening and she still doesn't know what to do. From time to time she still keeps shouting, as loud as she can; no answering call comes now . . .

Max Frisch

He's left the stove, filled with water; beside it are eight matches and half the box, so that she can strike them, some fuel as well and half the tin of coffee; his map and a compass are there too.

It turns into a beautiful, warm and cloudless day; you can see the sun penetrating deeper and deeper into the valleys, sending its slanting shafts of light through the morning air, with the veils of spray from the waterfalls glittering like silver or glass, and then you can hear the peaceful tinkling of the herds of cows coming up from somewhere in the valleys, a high, thin sound that keeps being borne along by the wind . . .

*

But for Irene, who only finally started out on her lonely way after a long wait, there comes a difficult and stressful time, a long and anxious evening outside the mountain hut, where she hopes, in vain, to see him return at any moment, then a sleepless night, during which she can't stop herself going over all the things that might have happened. And during which she reproaches herself for things which don't make any difference to anything. Perhaps she shouldn't have left the tent, she sometimes thinks, she should have climbed after him, right at the start, or she should have run down into the valley to fetch help, without wasting time, she should have done everything differently, just not lie in this hut waiting—!

84

The warden didn't even take his pipe out of his mouth when Irene told him, almost breathlessly, what her companion had set out to do. Irene probably thought he would go down that very evening and bring up a rescue party; in fact all he did was pick up his binoculars and look to see if anyone was stuck on the glacier, then said they'd just have to wait. He didn't even say whether or not he was afraid there might have been an accident. He just made the soup, as he'd done two days ago, when they'd sat together at the same table, and it made no difference that Irene sobbed once. We'll just have to wait, he said, at least until the morning.

And in the morning, when you wake up and remember everything that just for a moment you thought was only a bad dream, and when you are forced to acknowledge that twenty-four hours have already passed, that you still haven't done anything—

Irene is distraught.

It's eleven o'clock before the warden finally makes up his mind, takes his empty rucksack and sets off down to the valley to see whether they can get a search party together that day.

Irene leaves the hut too that day and goes up in the direction of the Ochsenjoch, at least part of the way to the col, together with young Barbara, who has been in the hut since the day before yesterday. And in a mountain hut, especially under these circumstances, you cannot avoid getting to know each other. Naturally it was very different from what both of them perhaps imagined. It's not just as if they'd known each other for ages; it's as if they knew no jealousy even, no hatred and no distrust, just their shared concern for the lost man, the shared torment at wanting to do everything for him and not being able to do anything. Not a word is said about who has lost him, not even on the walk to the Ochsenjoch together. Perhaps they look at each other now and then, when the other doesn't notice, when the other happens to be looking through the binoculars, or is pondering while they're sitting on a stone, waiting and waiting, and it may be that Barbara can't bring herself to ask a certain question, a question she would be ashamed to speak out loud. Every moment she can feel that Irene loves him too and perhaps she's always thought that she couldn't stand a woman who loved the same man, that she would have to hate and spit at such a woman. But things always turn out differently than you think, and it's comforting for Barbara when she senses how anxious Irene is for him, how Irene would like to do everything to see that he's rescued and it's as if it's precisely this same love that reconciles the two women to each other. At least as long as the man isn't there. And who knows whether he will ever come between them?

Evening has come again before the men the warden has brought up from the valley finally appear . . .

They saw them an hour ago, on the glacier that they crossed without ropes, and then it seems ages before they finally come up the scree slope; they seem to walk very slowly because they take very long, very calm steps, without haste, without slipping and without wasted exertion, almost effortless even though they have heavy heavy loads on their back, they look like large bundles of wood. And as they come closer you can see that they're not panting, just smoking their pipes. They have hard, brown faces and as they pass the two women, they just nod; only the warden wishes them a good evening as, one by one, they go into the hut where they deposit their ice-axes and bundles.

Irene and Barbara, however, who had perhaps imagined the arrival of these welcome rescuers would be different, more effusive, perhaps, and more solemn in a way, stay outside the whole evening, even though it gets very cold, and sit together on the bench by the wall, as if they'd been banished from the hut, which is now full of strange steps, strange voices . . .

Only once does one of them come to speak to them. It's the mountain guide who was always in the inn and who once said to Irene that he wouldn't go to bring anyone down from the North Ridge again. And now of course he's there in spite of that. He came out and had a look at the weather, which he clearly doesn't like the look of, and then he asks where the young gentleman started his ascent of the North Ridge? Unfortunately Irene can't tell him anything useful. Then he wants to know whether or not her companion perhaps had a lamp with him? To which Irene replies yes. And was he wearing that greenish costume he always wore in the inn? Irene can say yes to that as well; as she does so she keeps her eyes on his face to see if he is encouraged by her reply. But he just stands there, resting his foot on the balustrade with his brown hat on his head, and finally he just says they will set out in the morning and start by scanning the north side. Then, after he's put his pipe back in his mouth and after he's spent a while looking at the western sky, where there are no clouds but a dull, rust-red haze, as if someone had smeared their finger over the evening, he goes back into the hut.

Again and again Barbara keeps asking Irene to tell her what his final words were. And while the girl seems more and more anxious, Irene now feels a great calm, though she has no idea where she gets this calm; presumably it's simply her duty, because she's older, and it's as if the duty automatically brings the strength with it. Sometimes you might almost thinks she's Barbara's mother, it's so good when she strokes the desperate girl's hair. When she does so, there's no guilt and no reproaches, there's just life, which is sad and which you have to put up with nonetheless, whatever happens. Then you can sense that she's had to put up with a few things herself already and has a right to be calm like that. She doesn't tell Barbara everything he said during the last few days, for it's perhaps not always really best simply to tell the frank and open truth, especially when the truth is past and done with by then. But she tells her a lot, and she tells it in words which give off a soft glow, they way you talk about the dead, or at least about people whom we have lost—

Inside, the men from the valley have already lit the candles and they're drinking a last glass of wine; they don't get together often during the year and they tell each other this and that, slowly and deliberately, about the hay harvest they've had to leave in the middle of the work, and about their animals and the forest that was destroyed in a big landslide in the spring.

Outside, however, above the glaciers and the snow-fields, it's turning into a cold, windy night; the thin moon has a halo and the rocks look black in front of the milky bank of cloud, black and disembodied. And in the glaciers, lying there mute in this pale moonlight, the crevasses yawn and gape like wide-open fishes' mouths; the snow on the rock faces shimmers, as if you could see the cold, and it's all so immense when you think that there's a person out there, somewhere on one of those cliffs where there's no going forward or back, only this deathly cold in the space all round. On such a night it's as if God were showing a different face, a truer face, perhaps, that knows nothing of mankind and that shines without mercy, without pity towards life, so mute and stiff, so stony and alien, serious beyond measure, and Barbara bursts into sobs and it's a long time before she can suppress them, even though Irene comforts her and wraps her up in the blankets, the way she was taught, and even though she doesn't put out the lamp, so you can't see the night-dark mountains through the window . . .

The men set out while it's still night, around two o'clock. You heard them, even though hardly a word was spoken; just one of them cursed the weather. And indeed, when morning approaches it has clouded over, clouded over completely, and not a single peak can be seen, just the rock faces disappearing in the grey mist.

It's Irene who lights the fire, puts on the ice-cold water and sets the mugs on the table. What a loud noise it makes when you put the spoons in the mugs. Otherwise all you can hear is the crackle in the stove or the clatter of her heavy wooden clogs, and the wind, too, now and then, whistling in the chimney, and each of them knows what the other is thinking, even if neither says it out loud:

It's the third day now—

Outside the door, where you go to get wood, the stone flags are very wet; it rained during the night. And you have to assume it will have snowed higher up, if only a thin layer. Sometimes you can see the white when it clears for a moment. Down below, however, where new clouds of mist rise all the time and you can hear the roar of swollen streams, the wet rocks look like shiny black coal and the glacier is grey, as if smeared with ash, just in the great clefts and crevasses is there a shimmer of green, like bottle glass.

Later they washed and dried everything, including the crockery the eight men left. Then Irene gets the brush and gives the floor a good sweep while Barbara just sits on the bench, shivering and waiting . . .

And after Irene has shovelled up the dirt in the dustpan, taken it outside and thrown it over the cliff, she also cleans the pan that's been used, which actually wasn't really necessary, and later she even takes the axe and has a go at chopping wood, not worrying about the girl, who's still sitting on the bench watching, shivering and not saying a word, her hands in her pockets.

Does she believe they'll really find him? Barbara asks at one point and you can hear that she, Barbara, hardly believes that any more. Even when Irene says all sorts of things are possible: perhaps he spent the previous night back in the tent, perhaps he made his descent on the other side and is already somewhere down in the valley, in a hay-barn somewhere perhaps, or even staying with a shepherd . . .

Yes, perhaps.

But of course belief doesn't come from the head, and Barbara's heart is in no state to believe. It's full of memories of the last time they were together; of that stupid quarrel such as is quite possible between fiancés. And she spent the whole night lying awake trying in vain to work out why they quarrelled, why? All she can see is his eyes, the way they were at the end, so angry, and she can hear herself slam the door, and now she knows she can perhaps never make it up again . . .

91

After a long time waiting in silence she says, still watching Irene busy with the housework:

'I presume you really loved him?'

But Irene doesn't answer immediately; now she has sat down at the table and is cleaning the wick of the big lamp. She doesn't say that she didn't know about a Barbara, or whatever. Nor does she talk about her own situation, but just about him. That he was a good man, much better than he perhaps thought himself, and that he would have deserved a happy life. If you think, she goes on to say, of all the sick people there are, who can't have a life, then you feel like going and helping all those who are healthy and who can have a life but despite that don't for some imagined reason, yes, it's often difficult with healthy people, and yet he was a person who would have loved to have a life and could have, if he'd simply lowered his demands and been a good, happy person, who certainly deserved to be really loved—

Then, when she's finished cleaning the wick, she hangs the lamp back up on the big beam where there's a hook:

'Or wasn't he?' she asks softly . . .

But Barbara, who's said nothing the whole time, just keeps staring at her shoes: she, Barbara, has never really loved him, she then says, and she doesn't even change her posture when her friend turns round in surprise, no, she doesn't take one word of her confession back and whatever her friend tries to persuade her or dissuade her of, it makes no difference, after all she knows better:

Even the previous evening, she says, she only cried because she thought he was doing it to spite her. She was crying because she felt abandoned, yes, that's probably the way it always had been, all those years. She'd always seen everything he did or didn't do in relation to her own life, always judged everything by whether it made her happy or sad. If he happened to be ill, it was her misery, her misfortune, her annoyance that she had to go to the concert without him, when people praised him it was always her happiness, her pride, her joy that she had such a man. Everything he went through was for her delight or her distress. As if every person didn't have their own destiny that belonged to them, to them alone, as if they'd only been born just for our sake, as if they lived just to make us happy and suffered just to make us sad, as if they died just to make us mourn . . .

It is only after a long silence that Irene sits down beside her, puts her arm round her shoulder and says:

'But now you do love him—'

And it's probably not easy for Irene to say something like that, which gradually seems to make the despairing girl light up.

Now all her hope returns, new hope flaring up, as if everything must change for the better, since she feels changed and the same questions return a dozen times during the long day the two women spend in the cold, empty hut:

Perhaps he did really spend the previous night in the tent? Perhaps he really did descend on the other side, where it's easier, and is back down in the valley already? And perhaps he really is in a hay barn, or even with a shepherd who's given him hot milk, bread and cheese and a warm bed . . .

'Yes,' is all Irene says, 'perhaps.'

But Barbara is becoming less and less concerned with whether or not Irene believes it, and by the late afternoon, when the damp mist finally lifts, for Barbara there is no question any more but the certainty that they will bring him. She spends all the time standing outside the hut while Irene sits inside in a corner. Even the clouds sometimes part, even if the snow-covered ridges only appear for moments and then disappear in the greyness again and stay that way, at least there's a gleam now and then, somewhere among the clouds, that creeps across the glacier, a faint gleam, like brass or bronze, and you can say that the evening sun is filtering through, that there's a sun somewhere above the lowering clouds, a wide expanse of blue, even at this time and perhaps the peaks even tower up in a clear evening sky—

By now it's gradually getting darker and night has fallen by the time the warden returns.

Alone.

To their urgent questions about whether they found him, he just shakes his head as he replaces his ice-axe in the stand and takes off his wet things . . .

With the mist they naturally weren't able to do very much. They didn't hear any cries, either. They just found a rucksack. And when, later, he puts it on the table, there is no doubt that it is his rucksack. It was lying on the glacier, not far from the crevasse, but of course he doesn't say that. The rucksack appears to have fallen from a considerable height and probably on the first day, since it still contains almost all his food. The lamp's still in it as well, though completely smashed, and the warden puts everything on the table, also a knife and a black notebook which is swollen with damp, finally his leather purse too. And a watch, but unfortunately you can't tell when the hands stopped, so badly has the watch Barbara gave him been crushed.

So the other men are going to spend the night on the Ochsenjoch, even though, having found his lamp, they can't expect a distress signal, and tomorrow they're going to abseil down into the crevasse, another group is going to climb up onto the ridge and check the rock faces, as far as the new snow allows, and if they don't find anything then, they'll come down and wait for better weather, especially since, after four days, there's no hope of still finding him alive.

Barbara only starts to cry when she's lying on the sleeping platform; she's lying on her back, her arms alongside her body, so she's quite still and her crying is almost inaudible, not a word is said, not even when Irene bends over the motionless girl and kisses her, maternally, almost giving her her blessing, on her lips and forehead and eyes—

But outside, the mountains stand there as if nothing has happened; the Milky Way flickers as ever, a dusting of countless stars, and the streams coming down from the glaciers murmur in the silence, murmur without end.

*

It's towards three o'clock in the morning when they hear the scrape of nailed boots on the stones outside; shortly after there's a crash, as the door is simply flung open, and the clatter of an ice-axe falling on the floor—

Then silence again.

Irene jumped up, without shoes on, and Barbara is still awake as well, but it's some time, as if she can't stand up, as if she has no strength, as if the dark fist of the shock is keeping her on the sleeping platform. Only when she hears Irene's quiet cry does she take the lamp and light her way down the stairs . . .

He's standing there in the flickering light, which dazzles him, casting deep shadows across his face, and his eye-sockets are like black holes, and he stands there like someone risen from his coffin.

But he's alive—

He is alive. He bends down and picks up his ice-axe. He ignores the amazement, the questions, the tears of the two distraught women and goes into the kitchen as if nothing had happened.

Is there some hot tea? is his only question and then he tries to help at the stove. With his left hand. But the two women can manage now, although they're still quivering with fear and astonishment, and go about making the tea as if in a dream . . .

He also ignores the fact that his Barbara is there; he just sits down and then pulls his jacket collar open, while Irene puts some firewood in the stove and fans the flames and also pours water into the pan she cleaned, and while Barbara still stands there, as if she can't believe it, still holding the flickering lamp, as if it couldn't be put down on the table.

Then the fire is crackling and everything feels warmer, but you can't tell what he's looking at, the way he's sitting there; in fact it's almost impossible to recognize him, not only because of the beard he's grown and the shadows in his hollow, grey cheeks, and not only because his hair is sticking to his forehead, which is encrusted with dry blood, and because his mouth is so odd, so different, so thin and hard, with flecks of foam at the corners and on his lips. It must be something else that makes Barbara say such a strange way:

'So now you're back—Balz!'

Irene is standing by the stove staring at the water, where the first bubbles are starting to appear . . .

He only drinks the hot tea very slowly, he's holding the mug in his left hand and spills it several times. He doesn't want anything to eat; he shakes his head. He just lets a sugar lump dissolve in his mouth as he stares at the lamp close by him.

Later they tell him that people have been out looking for him, since the previous day, did he not see them, seven mountain guides—

He just says, 'Aha.'

His right arm is stuck in his jacket pocket, as if it doesn't belong to him, and he doesn't say why he doesn't take it out; nor how painful it is when a limb has frostbite. He doesn't say anything about what happened, not even that he looked death in the face and what he saw in it. He just sits there, and sometimes it's as if he's sleeping with his eyes open, or as if he's looking into the darkness, right through all the light, and is once more staring . . .

'Drink your tea,' Irene says, using the formal *Sie*, and he does and he's hardly aware that at once they used the familiar *du* to each other.

Meanwhile the warden has come from his shed; he doesn't say much either, just greets the returning climber. Then he goes to the stove and puts some more wood in to make the room warmer.

Did he reach the top?

But he doesn't answer the question he's asked, just sips his hot tea, and for a long time all they can hear is the ticking of the clock. But it's easy to work out that he didn't come back over the Ochsenjoch or the others would have been bound to see him. And if he descended by the West Ridge, then he must have reached the summit, even if he doesn't reply, as if he hadn't heard the question, as if he didn't want people to know . . .

Later the warden lit a candle and put it in the red lamp, where the flame gradually gets bigger and brighter when he closes the damper, and then, when he goes out and hangs the lamp by the door, so that the search party can see it and will know the missing man's been found, it's time he finally went to lie down; though actually it won't exactly be lying down, more of a collapse as his body gradually realizes that the three-day, three-night struggle is really over, that he is safe.

Irene stays in her seat and it's Barbara who makes his bed, spreads out his blankets and arranges his pillows, just the way she learnt, and Irene also stays in her seat when Barbara takes off his frozen boots and leads him to his bed, when she finally picks up the lamp and it goes dark where Irene is sitting . . .

But he doesn't say a word to Barbara either, as she wraps him up in the blankets, and he doesn't even nod his head when she asks him again if he has everything he wants and when she wishes him good night . . .

Safe!—he can still hardly believe that it really won't be death coming over him out of the dark, just warm sleep! All he knows is how grateful he intends to be for everything that may come after this sleep. Grateful even when they've cut off his right arm, perhaps one of his feet too, grateful for everything that's left to him, and that includes his left hand, it can wear the ring and you can work with your left hand as well, once you've learnt to, work like other people, even be an entire father and a real teacher, even if he will perhaps never be able to say what he heard in the great silence; but whatever withstood this silence must have great meaning, and even if he has lost some things during these three nights, then only because they perhaps amounted to little and what is left to him will be a lot, since he now knows that there's no such thing as an ordinary life, a contemptible life, that you could simply throw away, and that everything that we truly fulfil is enough.

Then Barbara blew out the candle so that the whole of the hut is in darkness.

Only outside, beyond the little window, you can still see the stars, which are now growing pale themselves, and day will soon begin to break. The sky is like a big piece of blotting paper which is gradually sucking up the black ink of night. A new, clear day will dawn, a glassy brightness, a silvery, sparkling glow, when the sun rises once more over the silent mountains and over the valleys where there are green meadows and woods that smell of resin and mushrooms, and you will descend lower and lower, past the first barns with the tinkling of the black goats, where there are flowers again, glittering in the morning dew, and once more it will be a clear and not too hot day, a gentle and golden day, as if nothing had happened, a quiet and peaceful valley, where you pass through villages and see people again, who greet you, where the women are doing the washing in the wooden trough, where everyone is occupied and the men will be standing on the slopes out there cutting the rye, which has ripened by now, with swinging and softly singing scythes—

Yes, he did think of that as, exhausted and shattered, but without fear, with frozen and painful limbs, but with new longing and knowledge in his heart, he sank into a deep sleep.

That being granted the opportunity to live is an unutterably serious piece of good fortune and that there can surely be no emptiness when this feeling has really been won, if only once, this feeling of grace and gratefulness.

Afterword

Or does she call it life, he asks, when you watch your
beard and your fingernails grow?

A man places himself in a situation in which the proba-
bility of dying is greater than that of surviving. Russian
roulette in the Alps. He's expecting a clean death or a
clean victory, but at the end there is neither—just a
maimed body and a mind that has had a brush with
madness. Back among other people, he is like a dead
man who doesn't know why he's still alive, speechless,
his eyes like black caverns and his mouth 'so odd, so different, so thin and hard, with flecks of foam at the corners and on his lips'. This image is more important
than everything else in this short novel—called a 'story'
in the subtitle. This image tells us that the only possi-
bility open to this thirty-year-old man, who has taken
himself to the very edge of his existence, is to be either
alive but dead or, as now, dead though alive.

Not to take this alternative seriously would be to
miss the point of the whole novel.

BIOGRAPHICAL BACKGROUND

A novel about a crisis in a character's life is never entirely independent of influence from the author's life. *Werther* is not, nor is *Death in Venice,* nor *Man in the Holocene,* each presenting a male crisis but at quite different stages in a man's life: Goethe's hero is twenty-three, Mann's is in his fifties and Frisch's in *Holocene* is seventy-three. Each case bears clear parallels to the author's life, but to simply enumerate the correspondences and dismiss the whole as 'autobiographical' would be a mistake. Goethe is evoking, in retrospect, the fatal variant of a crisis he managed to survive; the thirty-seven-year-old Mann is writing about a point in life that is yet to come; Frisch, still in full possession of his faculties, describes how, step by step, his solitary hero loses his hold on himself. In each case, the connection with the author's life has a different function. The diagnosis of 'autobiography' is thus never conclusive; what we must look for is the specific need to tell a story related to him- or herself at a specific point in the author's life.

Frisch made a radical change in his life at the same time as he finished this, his second, book. Abandoning his German course, he embarked on a technical career and began to study architecture at the Eidgenössische Technische Hochschule in Zurich (ETH, Swiss Federal Institute of Technology). He shook himself free, with great determination, of an existence entirely focused on literature and art. He had wanted to become a writer but this 'life in progress' was threatening to suffocate him. He thus escaped from the amorphous mixture of literary work and journalism into the cool rationality of architecture, to his 'love of Geometry' as he later put it in the subtitle of one of his plays. His father, with whom he had never got on, had also been an architect, though not a very successful one. His premature death five years ago, in 1932, had provided Max with a sense of release and, for a while, united him with his mother in an almost symbiotic relationship. Perhaps the course in architecture, which he resolutely completed, was an attempt at a personal reconciliation with his father, but there is no clear evidence to confirm this view. In *An Answer from the Silence*, it is the elder brother who assumes the paternal function. It is only in one place, strangely concealed, that we are told about the son trying to recover his father's walking stick from a mountain stream; we are not told whether or not he succeeded.

What is certain is that this book, with its conclusion hinting at a new approach to life, coincided with Frisch's decision to start a new life determined by architecture, by its clarity and rationality and characterized by a similar planned and conscious order. It was through architecture, after he had finished his studies, that he found his wife, Trudy von Meyenburg, the mother of his three children. This marriage was not only in line with the decision he had taken but it was also a significant social step—it was the entry of a young man, from a rather modest background, into Zurich's high society. The photographs of the time show an elegant bridegroom in a dinner jacket and white gloves.

FRISCH'S RECURRENT THEME

According to an article entitled 'Selbstanzeige' (Self-advertisement') that Frisch wrote in 1948 for his then Zurich publisher, it was a woman who provided the impetus for his change of direction in 1936. The sentence in which he reveals this is important for it both contains a key idea which shapes *An Answer* and throws up for us what may be regarded as Frisch's recurrent theme:

> Once, when a girlfriend and I were considering marriage, she said that I had not learnt anything which could be called a profession, and she wasn't wrong; also, she was only saying what I thought myself; but it was a shock, the first time I had seriously faced the fact that life can be a failure.[1]

If life is a failure then nothing can be done about it in retrospect, nothing at all. There is a terrible finality to it. In *An Answer*, this insight is expressed thus:

> All he knows is that there's no way of rectifying it once you've made a mess of your life, there's no going back, no making up for lost time and putting things right, no mercy; he knows, more clearly than he's ever known, that everything you do or don't do, every mistake and every omission, is final [. . .][2]

If my life is a failure, then it is I who have wasted it—no one else. I cannot blame either family or society or heredity. Nor is there a Providence secretly directing everything. Each of us have our life in our hands; we alone cause it to succeed or fail. Our destiny is always home-made—a conviction from which Frisch never departed.

There is a something cruelly inexorable about this insight—it subjects the individual to a daily judgement. The freedom of taking absolute responsibility for one-self is both wonderful and terrifying. *An Answer* is the story of a man who suddenly comes to understand this and whom the terror pierces to the depths of his inner-most being. Now he has to act—and it *is* a matter of life and death.

THE LIMITS OF A BIOGRAPHICAL READING

The woman mentioned in 'Selbstanzeige' was Käte Rubensohn, Frisch's lover since 1934. Their relation-ship foundered in 1938, when he was exactly halfway through his studies in architecture. Frisch blames the separation on the self-doubts that assail an older stu-dent surrounded by younger classmates:

> With time it became difficult to sit around as the senior among the almost boyish students, and the feeling of having missed my time gave rise to an infe-riority complex which distorted all values, confused every contact with the world. In quick succession all my human relationships foundered as well; they became impossible to the very extent to which one needed them.[3]

Here we stumble over the limits of a biographical reading of *An Answer*. Although Frisch's relationship with Rubensohn certainly had an influence on the novel, neither of the two female characters—the hero's harmless fiancée Barbara; and Irene, presented as a much more profound and enigmatic figure—may be directly related to or equated with her. With its compact plot, the story develops its own thrust and leaves behind all connection with the author's life.

To begin with, the main character, Balz Leuthold, thirty years old, Ph.D. and a lieutenant in the Swiss Army, in no way resembles the twenty-five-year-old Frisch, the eternal student who supported himself through journalism, writing delightful prose sketches as well as news articles. The hero, whose first name we only learn at the very end, is perhaps based more on Frisch's older brother Franz. It was Franz who had studied chemistry, completed his doctorate and then rapidly risen to the rank of lieutenant. But the hero's problems are alien to him—they belong entirely to Max.

As in the later *Holocene*, where he portrays a process of physical and mental decay from which he himself is far removed (warding off the catastrophe by putting it in writing?), here too Frisch describes a crisis in the life of a man who is five years older, who has an established position in society, who is an *homme de trente ans*. In so doing, he presents us with a double level of experience: the current one of the young author, who does not yet have an established mode of existence; and the future one of the man who has settled down in life. This doubling leads to a remarkable paradox that explains the problems that a reader may have with this little book. The end—the hero, shattered by his confrontation with death and humbled by his injuries—corresponds to Frisch's break with his aimless life as a writer and his move into architecture, into the conscious commitment of a regular profession, into marriage and fatherhood. And this is supported by biographical evidence. What precedes this ending, however, is a breathtaking analysis of the meaningless toeing of the line—of the trotting along with the herd; of the daily self-delusion with a secondhand meaning of life in which we believe only because others do too—a raging denunciation of a dreary existence which represses all our longings in our hearts, the lamenting and cursing of our dead lives in the supposedly divine ordained order, all this that blazes up so furiously at us out of the book is a vision that extends beyond the solution offered by the ending. *An Answer* is telling us about crises yet to come once this reconciliation with middle-class values is complete. The words uttered by the young man on the mountain top before lying down with his unexpected lover are more a cry than a question. One could call it Max Frisch's cry, a cry for all the years to come, to all the marriages, all the raptures and disasters of love: 'Why don't we live when we know we're here just this one time, just one single, unrepeatable time in this unutterably magnificent world?'[4]

This means that we must read the book in two ways. One, as a report of a man who finds himself—as a story of initiation, therefore, with many of the features of that genre. Confronting death and bearing thereafter the physical scars of that experience are also part of this age-old narrative pattern. Two, as opening up an area of conflict which can never be resolved and which cannot be eliminated even by the positive ending. This is the area of conflict which will be the source of all of Frisch's great works.

As far as his biography is concerned, however, we should add that for two years Frisch did no more literary writing; breaking furiously with the literary life, he even burnt large numbers of his drafts, diaries and fragments. But when the war broke put in 1939 and he had to join the army for a long period of military service, he found he could not survive the field-grey routine without his writing. He started off with diary-entry-like pieces which later appeared as *Blätter aus dem Brotsack* (Leaves from my Knapsack). This form of brief, freely composed sketches—a whole made up of fragments— was to prove immeasurably fruitful for his later work. The passion for language, that he had rejected, had caught up with him again.

HEROISM AND ITS CRITICISM

However, much of this early work is bound up with Frisch's whole oeuvre. No matter how much of his life, his loves and sorrows, is revealed and written down, each must be read as a story which develops and comes to a conclusion on its own terms.

The structure and composition of *An Answer* herald his future mastery. The crisis of the thirty-year-old hero is revealed to the reader step by step; literally, 'step by step', for walking, climbing higher and higher, is the central motion, is both action and symbol. And we soon realize that everything will be decided when our hero reaches the top. That is the 'goal' which appears in the text almost at the very beginning. It is settled, it has been decided upon.

We can very quickly deduce what that means from his mountain and rock-climbing equipment. It only gradually becomes clear, however, that it is the North Ridge he is heading for, a route that has never been attempted.[5]

For readers at the time, there was no doubt that the 'North Ridge' was an allusion to 'North Wall'. At the time of writing, the race to be the first to climb the North Wall of the Eiger was reaching its climax. An European spectacle, it was fired by Nazi propaganda— Hitler wanted a German to be the first. The first attempt in 1934 was called off after the death of one of the climbers. A two-man team died in the second attempt, in 1935; in 1936, a four-man team met with the same fate. Hence, the expression 'murder wall'. It was only in July 1938 (21–24) that a German–Austrian team finally met with success. In Germany as in Austria (annexed to Hitler's Reich for four months), this achievement was loudly trumpeted abroad.

Thus in 1937, when *An Answer* was pulished, the subject was highly topical. Since Frisch himself was an experienced mountaineer and rock-climber, he had firsthand knowledge of the subject. Given the fact that the world was breathlessly awaiting a triumphant ascent of the Eiger, the goal set by the young man for himself—in his attempt to escape a meaningless existence—is not an unusual one. And it is precisely this that makes significant the absence of any triumphant gesture at the end. There is no mention of a public response to the first ascent of the North Ridge; even the mountain guides merely shrug their shoulders—direct criticism of the contemporary cult of the hero, not least among the Fascists. One could argue that the cult's vocabulary does appear in the book—there is talk of a 'manly deed'[6] and of the alternative of 'the deed or death.'[7] But this line of discourse is not carried through; indeed, in the course of the story it is reflected upon and even criticized:

> It is his will that will send him to the North Ridge, to the deed or to death, as he used to say, and that despite the fact that he is clear, clearer than ever, that he doesn't believe in the deed. Even if he should reach the summit, will that make him a different person? Still, what is left but ambition to someone who has no longing any more, no true longing?[8]

The apparently heroic deed is a surrogate—it cannot replace the lack of meaning in his life; it can, at most, numb the feeling of emptiness. True meaning would be its own justification—it would remove all doubt, it would answer every question. Thus, as far as the book is concerned, the heroism of the manly deed, as fervently celebrated in the contemporary cult of the Eiger North Wall, is dead and buried. Yet the young man still sets off on the ascent of the North Wall.

Why?

Because he wants an answer. Now the title, which at first sounds almost clumsy, becomes important. But *An Answer from the Silence* is a paradox, like 'black light' or 'cold fire'. That which by its very nature cannot have voice is to speak, a silence that is the nameless other, that is beyond everything, that is 'perhaps God, perhaps nothingness',[9] 'a silence which gives you the feeling that it would kill you if you could really hear it'.[10] It is therefore no longer ambition that finally drives the young man up the North Ridge but his determination to challenge the metaphysical authority that must underlie all phenomena. At the extreme, face to face with death, it will speak. The journey to the limit, Russian roulette among the Alps, consists of staking your life for one single word, a word that really counts and makes it possible to say yes to life.

A LOVE STORY

One of the unsettling features of this story is that although it is also about love—the love between man and woman—this love is never accorded the ultimate redeeming force. Happiness is inconceivable without love, but the ultimate harmony fails to materialize—the combination of love, happiness and a meaning to life, a foretaste in the enraptured couple of the world perfected, the myth of the modern, post-Christian era. At the decisive point there is, instead of an explanation, simply a strange line consisting of nothing but dashes: a sign that what ought to be said here cannot be.[11]

Despite that, for the first time a utopia, which remains active in Frisch's writings, is here not only for-mulated but also lived out. It is the idea underlying his *Montauk* (1975)—to live out a fixed-term love, a full, real love which never turns into routine, a love without irritation, jealousy, satiety. A love 'without guilt'.[12] What is amazing is that it is a woman, Irene, who expresses this central idea. She formulates it with a precision, which has something final about it and which has never been bettered by the later Frisch. At night, Irene stands outside the young man's room and wonders whether she should simply go in:

> Perhaps it would be a very beautiful and very happy night; perhaps he wouldn't even ask what she want-ed and would just say he was expecting her or he was glad she'd come. Or they wouldn't say anything at all, just sit there together, with no questions or talk, which can only separate people. All he would know would be that she is leaving the next day and that they will never see each other again after that evening, and that knowledge would perhaps make their hearts freer than they had ever been, free of all

the past, that weighs down on us, and free of all the
future, that makes us hesitate, one evening that
belonged entirely to the present, to their real existence, and if they were to kiss each other, they would
know that it was their first and last kisses, and they
would perhaps be kisses such as they had never
known, words such as they had never heard, a happiness that was full of parting and can never become
shallow, can never become blurred by repetition,
one night, that only happened once, and perhaps
for her, for Irene, it would be even more, even more
than a significant memory, perhaps even the destiny
to which she had been called.[13]

It is striking that, after the opening, these reflec-
tions continue in one long sentence that will not,
almost cannot, come to an end for such is its emotive
thrust, a sentence that becomes a powerful, throbbing
whole precisely because it speaks of an incomparable
whole—the vision of an unbroken love.

And these two will indeed live out this love for one
day and one night, on the mountain top, where the
man takes the woman, and at the foot of the North
Ridge, in the tent from which he has disappeared by
morning.

Though it is the woman who seizes the initiative
and takes the morose and unapproachable man, an
independent, self-assured woman unconcerned with
official morality. The young Frisch shows astonishing
artistry in the way he builds up this character. Initially
all we see is a cliché, a pretty Danish woman in the

mountain inn, and expect nothing more. Then we are gradually surprised—for Irene uses her laughter and her bonhomie to conceal darker depths. It is only later that we learn the truth about her miserable life.

The moment of the electrifying meeting is beautifully set up. The man returns to a childhood game, and builds a little dam in a mountain stream in exactly the place where he had made one thirteen years ago. It is a strange, solitary activity and it is a while before he notices his onlookers. When he looks up, he sees Irene's face and is 'thunderstruck'. The air between them crackles with a sudden tension. It drives him to show off with a climb; later, it will lead to the woman deliberately taking the initiative. The love, that means infidelity for both of them, almost takes over his planned attempt on the North Ridge. It first rids him of his misconceived ambition, but then it strengthens his determination to demand an answer from the empty heavens. When he returns, everything is different for both of them. Their love remains the reality of one day and one night.

THE LONELINESS OF THE INDIVIDUAL

It is impressive how immune the twenty-five-year-old Frisch was to the dominant ideologies of his time. Given his fundamental existential homelessness and his trenchant critique of the falseness of the bourgeois analysis of the meaning of life, the clamorous slogans of those years could have proved very seductive. But he was not moved by any of them, neither by the glorification of nation and homeland nor by the international socialist movement, nor even by the Fascist promise of salvation any more than he was the Communists. And the criticism of civilization—widespread at the time and combined with the cult of nature and a natural, especially rustic, existence—was equally alien to him. He writes sympathetically about the work of alpine farmers but with no intention of setting them up as representatives of the healthy way of life compared to the ailing urban world. The central figure is alone in taking responsibility for his own life; he knows that it can fail and for the sake of his own self-esteem, he refuses to allow it to do so.

There are people who mock this early work, who call it regional because it is set in the mountains. That is as stupid as saying that Hemingway's *Old Man and the Sea* is a Cuban regional novel. A setting does not make an ideology. Such misrepresentations, especially in the 1970s with their rigid decree of what was or was not intellectually acceptable, could well be why Frisch distance himself from the story and chose to not include it in his collected works. The writing is certainly a long way off from the concise, terse style he was to develop in the postwar years, but in its radical outlook, in his refusal to hide from himself, this early work more than matches up to the later and late Frisch.

Peter von Matt

NOTES

1 Max Frisch, 'Selbstanzeige' in *Atlantis Almanach 1949* (Zurich: Atlantis Verlag, 1948), p. 97.

2 See p. 38 in this volume.

3 Frisch, 'Selbstanzeige', p. 98.

4 See p. 66.

5 Textual details indicate that the story is set in the Alps of the French-speaking Valais. However, writer and rock-climber Emil Zopfi has pointed out that the fictional landscape also includes elements of the Central Swiss and Glarner Alps, with which Frisch was familiar from his own moumtain expeditions. See Emil Zopfi, *Dichter am Berg. Alpine Literatur in der Schweiz* (Zurich: AS Verlag, 2009), p. 226ff.

6 See p. 8.

7 See pp. 8–9.

8 See p. 40.

9 See p. 22.

10 See p. 58.

11 See p. 81.

12 Max Frisch, *Montauk, eine Erzählung* (Suhrkamp Verlag: Frankfurt, 1975), p. 189. Translated into English by Geoffrey Skelton as *Montauk* (New York: Harcourt Brace and Jovanovich, 1976).

13 See pp. 41–2.